Dead Rites

Dead Rites Series

Markus Danielson

Published by Markus Danielson, 2023.

This is a work of fiction. Similarities to real people, places, or events are entirely coincidental.

DEAD RITES

First edition. October 13, 2023.

ISBN: 979-8223760962

Written by Markus Danielson.

Table of Contents

This this book is dedicated to my three angels up in heaven. My mom Alice, my friend Rachel, and my dog Gizmo. I miss and love you all.

In addition, this book is also dedicated to my dad, my sister, my brother, my brother in law, sister in law, my best friends and family.

Chapter One

1935 New York City, New York. On a cold and rainy October morning, former New York police detective, Daniel Benson, sleeps on his desk after drinking a bottle of whiskey. Benson, who is thirty-five years old, divorced, with a five-year-old little girl. Benson was a good detective who worked for the NYPD. He was set up by his former partner, Clark Young, who is now the captain of the NYPD. Now Benson is a private detective taking on shitty cases for little money. Daniel came from a family of police officers. His great grandpa was a police officer, along with his grandpa, and dad. One day his dad went to work and never came back. Benson's mom died when he was born so he was raised by his dad and his sister Valerie. So now when he works a case, he always wears his dad's gun and fedora hat as a good luck charm.

As the rain was coming down the window on Benson's office, he sleeps and lives inside his work building apartment; his Secretary Pilar Soto walks into the office and sees Benson sleeping on his desk again. She grabs the empty bottle of whisky and slams it in the trash, waking Benson up.

SLAM

Benson is startled by the noise. She slams the trashcan on the floor, then he finally turns to see Soto. "What the hell are you doing here?" asks Benson.

"I work here and it's Monday so sober up." Pilar tells Benson.

He begins to rub his eyes and gets up from his seat to head straight to the bathroom to pee and wash his face. Also, to change clothes. The rain was still hitting the windows of the office. Following the rain was thunder and lightning.

"I thought you quit drinking?" Pilar asks Daniel with slight disappointment.

"Had company, didn't want to be a rude houseguest." He used a lame excuse.

Pilar just ignored him as she was cleaning and wiping off his desk. "I'm gonna make some coffee." Daniel just ignored her as he was washing his face and getting ready to shave his five-o'clock shadow.

Daniel asks, "Anything for today?"

Pilar says, "Yes, we got a case of a missing man. The wife is coming in."

"What's the client's name?"

"Deedra Beneviento."

Daniel stops what he was doing for a minute. "You mean the Deedra Beneviento from the Beneviento Oil Company?" Daniel asks Pilar.

"Yes, why do you ask that?" asks Pilar.

"You mean to tell me her husband went missing and she's asking for our help?" Daniel asks in disbelief. "She's coming all the way from New Orleans, Louisiana to come to us? I'm not even that good, I'm a shitty corrupt police officer, remember?" Daniel tells Pilar.

Pilar says, "Well apparently the cops from down south won't help because her husband is Black, and I guess we are closer and you're cheap."

Daniel shook his head as he was changing into a new shirt, pair of pants, and a tie. "What time is her appointment?" Daniel asks Pilar.

"Eight thirty." Pilar says as Daniel was still in the bathroom. He opened his bathroom window to smoke a cigarette really quickly.

"Are you smoking in there?" she asks Daniel.

He sighed and tossed his cigarette out the window. "You never let me do anything. Why did I hire you again?" asks Daniel.

"Because I said yes and you needed someone to keep you on your toes since your divorce," answers Pilar.

Daniel was gonna say something but then there was a knock at the door. Both Daniel and Pilar ran towards their desks. Daniel closed his office door before jumping into his seat.

Chapter Two

As the door opened, Pilar sat at her desk and the look on her face was shocking. She rang Daniel to let him know his client was here. When he heard the knock on his door, he told her to come in.

He was in his office facing the window when his client walked into his office. He turned around to greet his client. Benson says, "Ah you must be my client, Deedra Ben..." he saw what she looked like and couldn't imagine how tall she was. She was all in black. Black dress and hat with the Vale, holding a black umbrella. Daniel's dad would once say, "She's a tall glass of water."

"Sorry, you must be Deedra Beneviento." says Daniel.

"That's Lady Beneviento!" Deedra says with her southern accent.

"Sorry," says Daniel "What can I do for you Lady Beneviento or Miss Beneviento?"

Lady Deedra says with her accent "Well I'm sure you've heard about my husband's disappearance, Roman Beneviento of the Beneviento Oil Factory?"

"I have, but I need more information. Like when he disappeared? How and why? When did you last see him?" he asks Lady Deedra.

Lady Deedra says, "It was two months ago. We had just celebrated our wedding anniversary. We have been married for three months, and he says he had to go away on a business trip. He hasn't been back since. He was supposed to come back a few weeks ago and nothing. The police officers won't help me because my husband is black, and they are very racial profilers down there." Lady Deedra continued. "I asked all the best detectives from Los Angeles, Chicago, and Boston and they won't help me. You are my last and only hope you will help me."

Daniel stared at her for a minute and said, "To be honest with you, I'm a shitty detective but I'm good at finding murderers and kidnappers. My charge is one hundred dollars an hour and I can start tomorrow morning. Just give me a picture of what he looks like and where he was seen last."

She dug into her purse and handed him a picture of her husband and a piece of paper of where he was going. Daniel looked at the train ticket. He was supposed to come to New York. "Thank you, kindly mister Benson. By the way, do you have a light?" she asks Daniel. Daniel was fumbling for his lighter to light up Lady Deedra cigarette. She got up, went to her purse again and poured money out. She gave him almost a thousand dollars in cash. As she got up, she started walking towards his door.

Daniel was mesmerized by how she was walking. It seemed like she was walking to the beat of a drum. He tells himself, "She has an ass like the devil and a face like Joan Crawford." Even Pilar was mesmerized by how she was walking. Pilar got out from her desk and went to Daniel's office. He was still amazed at how tall and how her walking got to him. Then Pilar snapped her fingers at Daniel to come to earth.

"You, okay?" Pilar asks Daniel.

"Humm. Oh yeah, I'm ok for some reason she gave me a thousand dollars in cash. Put it away but let me get a few hundred out of there." Daniel tells Pilar.

"You're not gonna drink or get cigarettes?" Pilar asks Daniel.

"No, you know when I'm on a case I don't drink or smoke on the job and besides I'm gonna go see my daughter and get her a gift," says Daniel.

As Daniel was grabbing his coat and hat, he was about to leave the office, he tells Pilar, "Be back in thirty minutes." As he left the building, it was still raining. He did lie to Pilar. He planned to head to his sister's bar just a few blocks away.

When Daniel walked into his sister's bar, he sat right at the bar table and waited to be served.

"Early morning already brother." Valorie says to him.

"Nah, just some eggs and bacon and a shot of whisky," says Daniel. His sister was taking his order. He got his shot of whisky and was about to drink it when he heard a familiar voice coming from behind him.

"Well, well, well, isn't it New York's finest private eye?"

Daniel ignored that statement. It was his former partner and New York captain, Clark Young with his three stooges; Paul, Chris, and Bill. "Looks like you're drinking the day away. Don't you have a case to solve? Like whom killed the cockroach or find some old lady purses?" Clark insults him.

"Leave my brother alone. He just came for breakfast." Valorie defended Daniel.

"Now Missy you don't talk to a lawman like that. Don't you have something to do, or do I need to put some people behind bars? By the way, you're late for rent." Clark tells Valorie.

She went to the back of the bar to get the money for this month's rent. Clark and his stooges are corrupt and like to take money from small businesses for protection. Valorie came back with some money and handed it to Clark.

"Thank you, kindly little lady," says Clark as he handed off the money to one of his stooges. He went to Daniel, and they looked at each other eye to eye.

Chapter Three

"I heard Lady Deedra Beneviento went to your office and hired you to look for her husband. Let me tell you something boy. She may have hired you, but no one, and I mean no one's gonna look for her dead husband. So why don't you play along and tell her to go back home so you can become homeless and not work anymore. Or just move to California, Chicago, or Boston. But they won't hire you either because I won't allow it."

Daniel just turned around and he finished his shot of whiskey and told Clark, "Too late. I took the job and when I finish this case, I'm gonna stick it up your ass and then I'll go to the police chief and tell him what is really going on with you. Don't fuck with me or my sister's bar. I may not be on the force anymore, but that don't mean I won't kick your fucking ass right now." he tells Clark as he was turning around to motion Val to get him another shot of whiskey.

"I wish you never said that boy. Officers arrest this man for threatening a police officer and public intoxication." Clark tells one of his stooges.

Paul comes up to Daniel. "Let's go!" As he was getting close to Daniel.

Daniel saw half a bottle of beer sitting on the bar. He stopped and told Paul, "Hang on. Let me finish this here beer." Daniel grabs the beer and chugs it along with the rest of his shot. He was still holding the beer bottle when he was finished, and he smashed it into Paul's head. Then Chris came after Daniel. He tossed Chris over the bar. Daniel grabs Bill and he punches him. He then headbutts Clark. Daniel then leaves the bar to go back to his office.

A few moments later, he came back to his office and started to get his stuff ready for his new case. "Pilar if that idiot Clark shows up, tell him I left to work on my case. I now have an arrest warrant for me."

"What the hell happened?" Pilar asks Daniel.

"I can't get any breakfast without any peace at my sister's bar." Daniel tells Pilar.

"So, you lied to me about leaving?" Pilar asks Daniel.

"I'm sorry I lied to you, but I did what I had to do, ok but cover for me please?" he tells Pilar.

Pilar asks, "Ok where are you going?"

"I'm going to New Orleans for my case, but first I have to see my daughter," he tells Pilar.

After he got done packing his luggage and his guns, he went to his ex-wife's house to see his daughter. He got gifts prior to seeing his daughter. He then walked up the front steps and he knocked on the door.

His ex-wife Rebecca answered the door. Rebecca whose hair was like wild fire color and had the greenest of green eyes she has whose parents came all the way from Ireland and was married to Daniel for almost ten years. Until Daniel lost his job and started drinking. They were both happier now.

"What are you doing here?" Rebecca asks Daniel.

"Nice to see you too, but I'm here for peace okay. I know I messed up and I'm sorry, but I have a big, big case and I'm going away for a while. I just want to see Leah to give her a present. Please let me see her. I don't want to fight or argue with you. I just want to see her before I go." He pleaded with Rebecca.

"Leah, daddy is here for you." Rebecca says in her thick Irish accent.

Leah hurried down the stairs with her pink dress and pigtails. "DADDY!" She was overly excited to see her dad.

Daniel reached out for her and held her up. "Hey you. I got some gifts for you." he put Leah down "Close your eyes." Leah closed her eyes "Okay, open them."

Leah opens her eyes, and Daniel holds out a few dolls and teddy bears.

"Thank you, daddy, I love you!" Leah tells him.

"I love you too honey!" Daniel tells Leah. Daniel then looked at Rebecca. "Here." he handed her money.

"You don't have to do this. Keep your drinking money." Rebecca tells Daniel.

"I stopped drinking. I've got a big case. I know I was a shitty person, but you know I'm good at finding the kidnappers and the killers just by looking at the victims. I'm going to New Orleans. Do you know the name, 'Beneviento Oil Company'?" Daniel asks Rebecca.

"No"

"It was run by Roman Beneviento. His wife came in to ask me to help. I got paid one thousand dollars. He was supposed to head up here but never made it. I'm gonna go to New Orleans to start there and see where his trail ends." Daniel continued. "If you need more money Pilar, has it. Just go to the office. I will let her know." Daniel tells Rebecca. They hugged each other because they all still cared for each other. "I gotta go. I'll call you when I get to New Orleans, I swear to you I won't drink. I want to work things out again with me and you for Leah's sake." Daniel tells Rebecca.

He opens the door, Rebecca and Leah behind him. He turned around and hugged and kissed Leah and hugged Rebecca again and then he stopped a taxi to head to the train station.

After the taxi dropped off Daniel at the train station, he got a one-way ticket to New Orleans. His train didn't leave for another thirty minutes so he called Pilar to give her some information.

"Hello, private detective Benson's office. Can I help you?"

"Pilar, it's me, Daniel. I need you to do me a favor."

"What is the favor?" she asks.

"If Rebecca shows up needing that cash, give it to her and if that pissass shows up tell him I left town." Pilar didn't say anything on the other end of the line. "Hello? Hello? Pilar you there?"

"Oh, she's here but she won't be for long. Now I know where you are going? You wanna call me a pissant? Then get ready cause you're gonna love this. Boys uncover her mouth."

Pilar starts screaming. "No please don't. I have a little boy at home. Do..."

BLAM

BLAM

"Guess what Daniel? You are now wanted for murder. See you at the train station." Clark says to him.

Daniel got pissed and says, "YOU MOTHERFUCKER! YOU BASTARD! I'LL KILL YOU MYSELF!"

Clark hung up the phone.

Daniel tried his best to hide before Clark and his stooges got to the train station but there were a few police officers at the station already. He heard the call come across their radios.

"Calling all cars and units. Calling all cars and units. There has been a murder at Skybridge building. Number five. Deceased female, late twenties. Suspect is former New York Detective Daniel Benson. Age 35. Black hair, brown eyes, five foot ten inches. Believes to be heading to the New York train station. Considered to be armed and dangerous. Please approach with caution."

Daniel went back to the payphone to call Rebecca to warn her about Clark.

"Hello?"

"Hey, it's me. Don't answer the phone or the door. I've been set up for murder. Clark killed Pilar. Don't even go to the office. Please babe, you got to believe me."

She paused for a minute. "Okay, I believe you. I know you wouldn't do anything like that. I always knew he'd set you up one day. Just go and come back in one piece please." she tells Daniel.

"I promise. Give Leah a kiss for me." Daniel hangs up the phone and tries his best to hide.

Chapter Four

Daniel ran to the men's room trying to figure out a plan on how to get on his train without getting caught. He peeked out of the door and noticed nothing but police officers in the train station. A few minutes later here comes Clark, and his stooges walking up. Daniel closed the bathroom door as he was still trying to figure out a plan. He went to the bathroom stalls to hide, when he noticed the bathroom door was opening. He figured he was caught, and it was over for him. He cracked open the stall door and it wasn't the police officers. It was a homeless person. Daniel opened the stall door all the way and he saw the old man. "Hey, pops, you wanna make a few bucks?" The old man nodded his head and Daniel tells him "What size pants do you wear?"

Another few minutes later Benson and the old man came out of the bathroom and went their separate ways. The homeless man went to the left and Daniel to the right. Daniel kept his head down and acted like he was drunk. The police officers were whistling to the other police officers saying they caught Daniel and here comes Clark and his stooges.

"Now I've caught you Daniel, you thought you were gonna get away with murder? Say goodby..." Clark paused for a minute. He turned around and yelled at all the police officers, "You are fucking idiots! This is not Daniel! It's just a homeless bum!" Clark asks the homeless bum "Where did the guy wearing these clothes go?"

The bum just says, "I don't know, he just gave me money to trade clothes with him and we went different ways."

Clark dropped the homeless guy and yelled at all the police officers, "LOOK OUT FOR BENSON! CHECK EVERYTHING! EVERY TRAIN! EVERY BATHROOM! I WANT HIM ARRESTED AND FACING HIS JUSTICE!"

Meanwhile, Daniel was almost on his train when the conductor stopped him. Daniel showed him his ticket and the conductor didn't let him on saying he stole the ticket.

"I didn't steal the ticket. I traded clothes with a homeless man. Let me on this train! It's a matter of life or death. I'm a private detective please," Daniel begged the conductor before the conductor could say anything someone yelled.

"DANIEL BENSON TURN AROUND!" Clark ordered Benson.

Daniel sighs and turns around "Nice bruise I left you. Does it hurt?" he asks Clark.

Clark tells Daniel "Cut the shit! You know what you did. We can do this the easy way or the hard way. Which one will it be?"

"Or can we do the third way?" Daniel tells Clark.

"The third way?" Clark asks with a confused look.

"Yes, you know what we used to do when we got bored at stakeouts? Showdown! First one to fire wins and you damn well know I got a fast hand. Remember? You used to call me quick draw Benson." he tells Clark.

"Fine! On three."

Clark and Daniel stared down at each other. Before either one of them got to fire, a hand came out of Clark's chest and ripped out his heart. Killing him instantly. The look on Daniel's face was shocking and before he knew it, he found more bodies. It was the stooges. They were killed too.

"What the fuck happened?" Daniel says to himself. The train whistle came on and Daniel ran to get on his train. The conductor saw what happened but didn't say anything to Daniel. He just punched Daniel's ticket and Daniel grabbed his briefcase and found his seat to sit down. He was finally going to New Orleans.

A few hours later he arrived in New Orleans, Louisiana. It was hot and muggy. A temperature of eighty-two degrees is unusual for October. The first thing Daniel did was get him some new clothes and then found a payphone to call Becky.

"Hello?"

"Hey, it's me. I made it to Louisiana. Shit went down. Clark is dead. I didn't do it. Something killed him." Daniel tried to explain to Rebecca.

"What do you mean something killed him?" Rebecca asks him.

"I don't know. I saw a hand come out of his chest and take his heart. Killed him and his corrupt partners. Look, I gotta go. I'm gonna find a hotel room and something to eat. Give Leah a kiss for me. I'll keep you updated." Before Becky could say anything, Daniel interrupted her. "Becky, if something goes wrong, go to my sister's place. Stay there, but it would be best if the three of you left. I love you all. I'll be home soon." Then Daniel hung up the phone.

Chapter Five

After finding a hotel and shop to get new clothes and a restaurant to eat. Daniel went to his room. He showered and tried to relax but couldn't because he knew he couldn't go to sleep without a drink and a cigarette. He tried to get some sleep as his mission was first thing in the morning. Daniel tried to sleep but every time he tries to go to sleep, he has nightmares. In his dreams he sees his mom being attacked and raped by some guy who is dressed in black. Whoever the person is, he always has blood on his chin and Benson's mom lays down and cries because she sees the blood on her neck. And that is when Daniel wakes up all sweaty and can't go back to sleep. That is why he always drinks his whiskey so much. He gets black out drunk. When Daniel got up in the morning he got dressed and got some breakfast and then after breakfast he went to the police station to talk to the captain that is in charge.

"Hello. I'm the New York private detective Daniel Benson. I'm looking into talking to your captain in charge here." he tells one of the officers at the front desk.

"That would be Captain Shepard. If you turn to the left side of the hallway, his door is the last one on the left. You can't miss it." the cop tells Daniel.

Daniel thanked the police officer, and he started walking to Shepard's office.

Knock!

Knock!

"Come in." A voice from the room tells him.

Daniel entered Shepard's office. "Captain Shepard. I'm private detective Daniel Benson. I came all the way from New York for a case I need your help with."

Captain Shepard says, "What kind of case?"

"The Roman Beneviento case."

Shepard had a shocking expression on face. "Why the fuck are you taking on this case boy?" Shepard asks angrily.

"Lady Deedra Benev...."

Shepard cut Benson off. "We don't say her name around this town." Shepard continued. "The only thing I can tell you is that ever since her husband went missing a lot of shit has been going on around here in my city of New Orleans." Before Daniel could say anything, Shepard handed Daniel a note. "Take this and get out of my office!" Shepard tells Daniel.

Daniel left Shepard's office and he opened the note on his way out. "New Orleans morgue. You'll find answers there. Ask for Joseph and Martha."

After Daniel read the note, he left the police station and headed to the morgue. After he hailed a cab and got to the morgue, he went inside the building. It smelled like dead bodies, and it was hot inside the building as well. He rang the bell and out came a female from the back.

"Hello, can I help you?" she asks.

Daniel says, "Yes, hello? I'm conducting a missing person investigation and the captain tells me to come here." Benson says.

"Well do you have the case number or name?" she asks.

Daniel says, "Yes, Roman Beneviento."

She took a long pause and said, "I'm Martha. My boss and I have been waiting for someone to come and help us with this case. Follow me." Benson came from around the desk and followed Martha. "You have no idea. We have been stumped on this case. No one is helping us, and we have asked so many police and private eyes and still nothing. They never showed up. Glad that you are here to help us," says Martha.

"I'm from New York, so long story, his wife or widow came to me asking for help and ever since I got here, I've been shot at, your police captain doesn't like me very much since I said that name, he's been acting like nothing happened," says Daniel. They were both walking to the back still till they finally saw the double door. The smells of the dead bodies were getting worse and worse.

"Boss, we finally have someone to help us with this case." Martha announces. Out comes a man who is six feet two, has glasses, and facial hair.

"Hello, sir, I'm Joseph. I run this morgue; can you help us?" Joseph asks Daniel.

"That is what I'm here for. My name is Benson. Daniel Benson, private eye from New York. What the hell is going on with this case?" ask Daniel.

Joseph says, "Well sir get ready for a shit show. Follow me." Daniel followed Joseph to one of the ice coolers; he pulled the door to open it and pulled out the tray of the dead body of a Black male in his forties. "Roman Beneviento. I presumed?" Benson questioned.

Joseph just nodded, and he tells Benson, "Get some of these gloves and a facemask and let me show you what we found."

As Daniel was putting on the gloves and facemask, Martha uncovered Roman to help Daniel with the clues on the body.

Martha says, "Okay as we can see, his body is all dried up like a big leech sucked on his blood. They left the body organs and parts and just drank the blood."

Daniel got closer to examine the body.

Chapter Six

"I see something! Bring the light over here!" Daniel tells Martha. Martha moved the light to where Daniel was pointing at. "See, look. This is why he was drained of his blood. Multiple holes on his thigh right next to where his penis is at. It looks like a big ass spider bite or a snake bite." says Daniel.

Joseph noticed something too. "Hey look at this." Joseph says. He was pointing to Roman's mouth. Martha shined the light on Roman's mouth, and you can see some pointed teeth that were beginning to grow but had stopped midway.

"What the fuck?" says Daniel.

"Wait a minute. Let me show you another victim." interrupts Martha.

They all went to the other icebox. Martha opened it and uncovered the blanket. It was the body of a female without her head.

"What the fuck?" Benson continued "Where the hell is her head?"

"We never found it with the body but from word on the street is, she is or was a prostitute. Here is her purse," says Martha. Martha was handing over the purse to Daniel, they both smiled, and he took the purse from Martha.

Daniel started to take the contents out of the purse. Lipstick, money, change, a hotel key, and her passport identification. "Jane Rose. Blonde hair, blue eyes. Five foot three inches and one hundred and ten pounds. From Canada." Benson paused for a minute. He remembers Jane. She was the one who broke off his marriage because Daniel wouldn't let her get her out of jail, so she set him up. It ended up breaking up his marriage to Rebecca. "Oh well, once a prostitute, always a prostitute," says Daniel.

"Does she have the same marks on her? Like with Roman?" Daniel asks Joseph.

"No. It's just that her head was ripped off. Whoever it is, they must not like prostitutes." says Joseph. Joseph began putting the body away. He then yells out to Martha and Daniel, "THAT'S NOT A WAY TO GET AHEAD IN LIFE!"

Benson tells Joseph "That was mean. I mean come on. Now is not the time to lose one's HEAD!"

After those jokes, Joseph put the bodies back.

"We were gonna call it a night."

Daniel asks Martha, "Is there a bar in town? I can use a drink if you'd like to join me?"

"Sure" she answers Daniel. "I know a spot." she says.

After she got her purse and locked the doors for the night. They both walked to a bar called 'Speakeasy'. Once they were inside, they found a seat and started drinking.

"So how long have you been a private eye?" Martha asks Daniel.

"For a year. I was a detective for the NYPD for ten years till my former partner set me up for something I didn't do." he tells Martha.

"Oh my god! That is horrible." she says.

"It got worse, he was named police captain and fired me. Cost me my marriage and my job. But you know what? It is what it is, and he got his karma." Benson tells Martha.

Martha got out of her seat and got close to Daniel and sat next to him. She opened up her small purse and got out her cigarettes. "Want one?" she asks Daniel.

"Why not?" He spoke. As Martha was lighting Daniel's cigarette the server came by and asked what they wanted to drink.

"Two whiskeys and two beers," says Daniel. As the server was getting the drinks Daniel and Martha talked more and more.

"How long have you been married?" Martha asks.

"Ten years but divorced." he tells Martha.

"Have any kids?" she asks Daniel.

"Yes, a five-year-old named Leah," he says.

"Are you guys trying to work things out?" She asks.

"I don't know I want to, but we will see after this case." Daniel tells Martha.

The more they talked, the more they drank, and the more they got really close to one another. A few rounds of drinks later and they were kissing, and they ended up at Daniel's hotel room to have sex. After they had sex, Daniel was having his nightmares again, but it was different. He saw a young woman being attacked but only this time the guy dressed in black turned around and pointed to Daniel and says to him, "You're next!"

Benson woke up in a cold sweat.

"What? What happened?" asked Martha as she was getting up and got close to Daniel.

"These nightmares. I have had them since as far as I can remember. That is why I drink. I become so drunk, I blackout and don't remember anything," says Daniel.

"Oh, my I'm so sorry I didn't know." Martha says as she begins kissing Daniel's arm. She hugged Daniel in the process. "Don't worry. I won't let that big bad person or whatever you have come get you." Martha tells him.

They both laid back in bed and went back to sleep.

The next morning Martha got up early. As she was getting ready to head back to the morgue. She looked at Daniel one last time, rubbed his hair and kissed him on the cheeks. She shut the door and left to go to work. A few minutes later Daniel got up feeling guilty about what happened. He is trying to work things out with his wife and daughter. After rubbing his face, he realized he forgot his shaver. He says, "Forget it," and gets dressed to go talk to Martha and explain to her about what happened.

A few minutes later Martha went to open the doors for work when she noticed Joseph's car was still there.

"That's weird. He never stays late." Martha tells herself. Once she opened the doors, she tried to turn on the lights, but they wouldn't turn on. "What the...." The only light coming through was from the back door.

"Hello? Doctor. Are you in here?" Nothing. "Doctor?" Nothing again. She was still walking towards the back. "Hello?" Then suddenly she heard a noise coming from the back like someone moaning in the back. She crept up slowly towards the back of the room and she peeked open the door and what she saw was disgusting. What she saw was Joseph playing with the head of the corpse of Jane. But what else she saw was that he had put the dead head of the corpse between his legs, and he was acting like it was giving him oral pleasure. She tried to leave but she knocked over a tray of tools and when Joseph turned around and heard that noise and saw Martha, he was a different person. What she saw was he had blood on his mouth and his eyes had changed color. They were like an animal's eye color. He also had fangs coming out of his teeth.

"Ah, fresh meat. Hey Martha, do you know what everyone says about me? I SUCK!"

Martha got up and started running towards the front door, but Joseph was already running towards her with the dead head still attached to him. Martha almost reached the front door, but it was too late. Joseph got Martha by the hair and was dragging her back. She was screaming and yelling for help, but it was no use, no one heard her. He tied her up and taped up her mouth. He then tells Martha, "Don't worry about it love. This will all be over soon. Once I get done with you, I'm gonna get that piece of shit private eye and soon both of you will join us. The goddess requests your presence." He was about to bite Martha right on the neck when the bell rang.

"HELLO?" It was Daniel.

"God damnit! Worst time ever. Oh well. I'll save you for dessert." says Joseph. He went back to his normal form and put the head right next to Martha. "Don't go anywhere. Both of you!" Joseph went to the front of the office.

"Hello mister Benson. Anything I can do for you?" he asks Benson.

"Yeah, I was just wondering if Martha has come in yet?" he asks Joseph. Before Joseph could answer Daniel, he saw some blood coming from out of the side of Joseph's mouth. "What happened to your mouth?" he asks Joseph.

"Oh, I must have bitten my tongue hard, but Martha is in the back if you would like to talk to her."

Daniel went around from the desk to follow Joseph. Joseph held the door open for Daniel. As Daniel was going first through the door, he noticed something. "Seems dark in here." Daniel continues, "Funny all the lights were on and now they are all off." He suspiciously tells Joseph.

"Old building sir." he tells Benson.

"Funny, the windows are blacked out too and the shades are not open up yet?" Benson questions Joseph again.

"I just got here sir." Joseph tells Benson as they kept walking to the back. Daniel stopped walking with Joseph right behind him. "Anything wrong sir?" Joseph asks Daniel.

"Blood. It looks fresh and medical tools are on the ground." Daniel turned around to face Joseph. Before he could question Joseph, Martha made a noise so loud that it made Daniel turn his head to see where the noise was coming from. Before he could find it, Joseph grabbed Daniel by the shoulder and when he turned his head Joseph went back to his evil form.

"WHAT THE FUCK!" Benson tried to punch Joseph in the face, but it was no use. He was so strong, and he grew taller than Daniel. A normal human punch didn't work.

Joseph just gave an evil smile and tells him, "MY TURN!" He picked up Daniel and tossed him through the wall and Daniel ended up in the next room. Benson went for his gun and started shooting at Joseph. The bullets didn't affect him. Joseph tells Daniel, "STUPID LITTLE HUMAN YOUR WEAPONS WON'T WORK FOR US!"

Daniel kept shooting at Joseph in the face till he let him go. "NOW YOU'RE GONNA PAY YOU LITTLE SHIT!"

As Joseph was going towards Daniel, he reloaded his gun, and he noticed how the sun was coming out. Joseph picked up Daniel again. "I'M GONNA SUCK YOU DRY!" Joseph tells Daniel.

BLAM

Joseph looked over at one of the windows.

BLAM again.

The window busted open, exposing the sunlight, hitting Joseph in his arm and letting Daniel go. BLAM! Wherever Joseph went, Daniel would blast the windows to let the sunlight in and put up the curtains as Joseph hid in the corner of the wall where there was no sunlight. Daniel got a wooden chair and broke it to get the sharp end of the chair.

"WHAT THE FUCK ARE YOU?" Daniel asks Joseph. As Joseph was coming out of the dark, Benson can see his skin all blistered, bloody, and smoking.

"We are the new world. We are the new world that will cleanse this filthy place, our queen, our queen, our goodness will lead us to the new world." he tells Benson. Joseph was going back to his normal self.

"Who is she? What's her name?" he asks Joseph. As Daniel got closer to Joseph he got ahold of Benson's hand where he was holding the sharp end of the leg chair. Joseph was bringing the sharp end close to his chest where his heart is.

He tells Daniel his final words. "FUCK YOU!" And then Joseph stabs himself in the heart.

Chapter Seven

As Daniel was still in shock about what had happened, he noticed a strange tattoo on Joseph's arm. "That's weird." he says out loud to himself. He needed to find Martha to find some answers.

"MARTHA!" he yelled. He could hear her making noises, so he followed the sound of her voice. "MARTHA!" He yelled repeatedly. She kept making loud noises till Daniel found her. "Oh my god! Are you okay?" He asks her as he begins untying her. He noticed the head of Jane Rose; he stopped while Martha finished untying herself. "It's a shame she wasn't HEADSTRONG anymore. Looks like she won't be HEADING home. You popcorn bitch!" Benson says jokingly. He spit at Jane's dead head and then he turned around.

Martha just got done untying herself.

"Are you okay?" he tells Martha.

"Yes, thank you. I'm glad you showed up. What happened to Joseph?" she asks.

"He's dead. What the fuck happened? What is going on?" he asks Martha.

"I don't know, but I'm just glad you were here. Another minute and I would end like Roman in the icebox there." She tells

Daniel. She hugged him and she was about to kiss him, but Daniel stopped her.

"Listen, about last night, I know it meant something to us but I'm trying to work on my marriage for my kid's sake. I came over here to tell you that, but now we have something. I'm gonna need your help now. Will you please help me?" he asks her.

"Yes, you saved my life so now I will return the favor. What do you want me to do?" Martha asks Daniel.

He replies, "First I want you to examine your boss in the other room and see what you can find. I'll be looking for clues. I don't know where to start, but maybe I'll start at his place." Daniel walked towards Joseph's body and started looking through his pockets. He found Joseph's wallet and opened it up. He found his driver's license which had his address on it. "Looks like he won't be needing these anymore." Benson was taking Joseph's car keys out of his pocket and was about to leave when Martha ran up to him and hugged him again

"Don't worry. I won't tell your wife." Martha tells Daniel before she kisses him on the cheek. She ran back to get started on the body of Joseph.

Daniel went outside in the hot humid weather of New Orleans. As Daniel was walking to get into the car, he started to feel sick and began to have a headache. He would usually get headaches, but none that would hurt him. He hurried into the car to get away from the sun. He started up Joseph's car and was heading towards Joseph's house, which was a twenty-minute drive. Meanwhile Martha, who was still in her nurse's outfit, all messed up from what happened earlier that morning. She took off all of Joseph's clothes and started looking for clues to what had happened to him.

About twenty minutes later, Daniel showed up at Joseph's house. His yard was not in good condition. Just in an okay condition. Crickets were still outside but fading away as the birds were starting to chirp outside. It was a small one-bedroom, white house. Once Daniel got to the front porch, He used Joseph's key to open the door of Joseph's house. Once Benson opened it, he could smell rotten meat, or a decaying body. Daniel pulled out his gun and started searching inside the house. He tried to open the blinds, but the windows had boards on them. The house was a complete mess. Roaches and mice were running all over the place. Dirty dishes were still piled up in the sink.

"Oh god, fucking nasty ass pig!" Daniel says after he checks the front room and kitchen. No clues, but he can still smell something rotting. As he went and checked the upstairs bedroom, he heard a noise in the basement. He hurried to the kitchen to see the basement door but unfortunately, there was a padlock on it and Benson needed to find the key. Daniel ran upstairs to see if he could find a key to the basement and unlock the door. He wanted to see if there was a survivor in there. He went to the bedroom and noticed the bedroom was a mess as well. The bed was not made, sweat stains on the bed sheets. He saw a small dresser beside the bed. He turned on the lap and when he opened the dresser drawer and he saw some papers with some weird writing and a book as well. Also, a drawing that looked like a weird knife or dagger. He put everything in the book, and he took it with him. Benson found the key to the basement door, and he hurried back downstairs. Once he reached the basement door, he unlocked the padlock and he opened the door, and it was pitch black.

"Motherfucker!" says Daniel. "Hello? Anybody down there?"

"HELP ME PLEASE!" screamed the voice of a female.

"HANG ON HONEY! I'M HEADING DOWN! ARE YOU HURT?" Benson yelled to the unknown female.

"DANIEL IS THAT YOU?" she yelled back to him. Then suddenly he recognized the voice coming from the basement.

"JENNIFER!" Daniel yelled.

"PLEASE HELP ME!" She tells him.

Daniel saw a lamp on the side of the basement door. He got it and lit it up and then he started to head downstairs. Once he headed down the last step, he saw what Jennifer looked like. She was bleeding from the neck, and she was bruised and blue. Her blond hair was covered with blood from her neck, and she was tied up. Her wrist was bleeding from struggling to get loose.

Daniel and Jennifer dated a few years back before he became a police officer. "What the fuck happened? I thought you went back to Missouri?" Benson tells Jennifer. Benson notices rotten meat of what looked like body parts and animal parts. "You sick fucker," says Daniel.

"I did! Then I got kidnapped and ended up here." She tells Daniel. As Daniel was getting Jennifer down from the pipes, she gave Daniel a hug. "Thank you! Thank you!" she tells Benson.

Daniel says, "Okay let's get you out of here. Can you walk? I know you are weak but help me out okay." As they were both walking upstairs Jennifer was getting weaker and weaker and weaker. "What did Joseph do to you?" he asked Jennifer as they both climbed the last step out of the basement.

"It wasn't him. It was her!" Jennifer nervously tells Daniel.

"Who is she? What do you mean by "she?" Daniel asks Jennifer.

Before Jennifer could answer she went down to the ground, and she started to act weird. She was crying and covering her face. As Daniel tapped her shoulder, her face changed like Joseph's did.

"OH FUCK!" yelled Daniel. Daniel tried to reach for the back door, but it was too late. She grabbed him by the leg and was holding Daniel upside down and they were face to face.

"Hmmm it's been a long time since I ate some fresh meat. Tell me something honey, I missed you and I want you! After I fuck you, I'm gonna suck the blood outta you. I'm gonna make you mine again." Jennifer tells Daniel. She threw Daniel on the front room floor as he was struggling to get up and get out of the front door, she kept changing more. Her eyes changed to animal eyes, her ears were getting to point, her fingernails were getting longer, and her teeth were getting fangs. She started charging at Daniel, but he was quicker than her. He grabbed her and tossed her towards the front door. The door busted open, and her body was now outside.

Once Jennifer was outside in the sun, she was begging to burn. She was making a sheik scream as her body was on fire. She was talking to someone, but Benson didn't see anyone else around. "YOU PROMISED ME! YOU PROMISED ME I CAN HAVE HIM! YOU LIED! YOU LIED TO ME! YOU BITCH!"

After her body was consumed by the fire, leaving nothing but ashes and smoke. Daniel went outside holding his thigh. Double checking to see if the body had turned to nothing, but bones and smoke and it was.

"This is why I stopped dating crazy ass bitches." he says. Daniel was starting to get another headache. He picked up his lucky hat and started to walk towards his car. It was time for him to head back to the morgue before something else crazy happened. As soon as he left, the police showed up at Joseph's house to see what happened.

Meanwhile at the morgue, Martha was doing an autopsy on Joseph just like she did with Roman. He too had two fang-like marks between his thighs, and he had what he looked like the same tattoo Daniel saw on Joseph's arm.

"What the hell?" she says.

Just then Daniel showed up at the back of the morgue. Martha noticed how he looked all bloody and bruised

"My god! what happened?" she asks him.

"Crazy ass ex that became something and was set on fire" Benson tells Martha as he was limping to her. She was trying to attend to his wounds, but he just shoved her away and just looked at Joseph's body "Did you find anything on this asshole?" Daniel asks Martha.

"Yes, he has the same marks as Roman did and I found this necklace around his neck."

Martha handed Daniel the knife, "Humm let's see what the notes and book have on it." As Benson was opening the notes and book and was about to see what the notes were, about then the doorbell rang. Benson and Martha paused and looked at each other.

"Hello it's Captain Shepard."

Benson collected all the notes and the book and hid. He knew the police officers were looking for him. As Martha was looking to see if the coast was clear, she went to the front of the desk to greet Shepard. Benson couldn't hear what was going on till he heard two voices coming to the back.

"So, you mean to tell me he just stabbed himself in the heart without a warning?" Shepard asks Martha. She just nodded her head. "Then if he killed himself, then who was driving his car?" he asks Martha. Martha just shrugged her shoulders while shaking her head sideways making no motion. "Is that private detective from New York still here?" he asks Martha.

"I don't know." she answers Shepard.

As Shepard was getting angry at Martha he says, "Well you know what? Why don't you be a doll and call the hotels and see if he is still here while I examine the body." Shepard tells Martha. As Martha was leaving, Shepard tells her, "And a cup of coffee. Black." She just nodded her head while she kept walking.

As Martha left, Daniel was hiding in the storage closet. He can see Shepard getting close to the dead body of Joseph. Then all of a sudden Shepard changed to what Joseph was, what Jennifer was but it was full Amerion. Shepard hissed at Joseph's dead body and started to talk to the dead body.

"You dumb bastard. You just had to get your rocks off with a head shame. Joseph, I told Akasha to leave you behind and leave you to turn you into stone, but she needs more minions." He continued. "Now we have a few more days for the queen, the great mother, to cleanse the world of filth. I'm gonna kill Benson myself before Halloween." He starts to rub Joseph's hair. "I'm glad you didn't kill him yet, because he doesn't know what he really is. The great mother will tell him after what she gets from him." Then with Shepard's claw-like hands he went to Joseph's chest and pulled out the rest of his heart and drank the blood from it. Then all of a sudden, he hears footsteps. "I'm gonna get this little bitch too." he says, then Shepard went back to his normal human form. "Anything Nurse Martha?" Shepard asks her.

"No, he must have gone back to New York." Martha tells Shepard.

"Okay then. I take my leave. If you see Benson or have any questions you know where to find me," Shepard tells Martha.

Martha was walking Shepard out when Benson stepped out of the supply closet shaking his head and startled. "What the fuck was that? And what the fuck does he mean by what the fuck I am?" he says. As soon as he said that Martha came back to the back room.

Chapter Eight

"Martha what the fuck is going on here in this town?" Daniel angrily asks Martha.

Martha paused for a minute, and she finally told Daniel the truth. "There has been a rumor going around that this town is full of vampires and I'm not a nurse. I really am a witch. A good witch and my Voodoo witch friend and I are looking for clues to stop the evil from spreading."

Daniel, who had a confused look on his face replied. "Vampires are not real. They can't be real. What I saw with Shepard, Joseph and with Jennifer, they didn't look like no goddamn vampires and secondly, if you were a witch, how come you didn't use your power or whatever on your boss and on Shepard?" he asks Martha.

She answered, "Come with me and we will explain everything to you."

He says, "How can I trust you at this point? I'm gonna have to sleep with one eye open and my gun under my pillow?" he tells Martha.

She paused for a minute and said, "I made you sleep with me. I didn't spike your drink or anything. I just wanted to sleep with you and go inside your head and I did." Benson, who has a shocked look on his face, started pacing back and forth "Just come with me please. I promise I won't go inside your head again." she begged Daniel.

"Fine I'll go with you but if you do something else, I'll turn myself in to Shepard." he tells Martha.

So, after they closed up the morgue building and they stepped outside, it was hot, and the sun was out. Daniel began to get more headaches. Even wearing his dad's hat and sunglasses, they were not helping, and he fainted.

A few hours later he came to, and he was inside a bedroom. It was full of witches, voodoo, and gypsy stuff.

"Ow my head!" Benson cried as he grabbed his head with both of his hands because that was how bad of a headache he had. He heard a curtain open up from behind him and it was Martha with some woman who looked like a gypsy.

Martha tells Daniel, "Hey love, how are you feeling?"

"Like I was walking in the hot Arizona desert, what the hell happened? And where am I?" he asks her.

"You're safe. Don't worry about it, okay? We are here to help you?" Martha tells him.

"Tell me right now! Who the hell are you or what are you?" Demanded Benson.

Martha finally tells him the truth. "We are powerful high witches and gypsies. We are here to help you and figure out what is going on. This is my friend Ronda Redhook. She is a high gypsy." Martha tells Daniel.

Daniel looked at Ronda. She must have been in her 80s. She has the scarf, the earrings, all legit like all gypsies wear when they come to New York for the world's fair every year.

Ronda came to Daniel. She grabbed his hand, and she started speaking French. After she got done doing what she was doing with Daniel. Ronda screamed.

"Are you sure?" Martha asks Ronda.

"We c'est un." she tells Martha.

Benson, who has a confused look on his face says, "Does anybody wanna tell me what is going on?" He asked both of them, they just ignored him.

"How many days till he has left?" Martha asks Ronda

"Deux Jours." she tells Martha in French.

"Hey, I'm right here, what is going on?" Daniel asks Martha and Ronda. Again, Ronda just went to the front and Martha stayed in the back to tell Benson the news.

"I hate to tell you this Daniel but, something bad will happen to you in two days at midnight when Halloween hits," Martha tells Daniel,

"What will happen to me?" Daniel tells Martha

"I don't know. I know I can speak French, but her French is really hard like she is scared of you. She won't even talk to you or look at you. She just tells me to let you know to get out of her shop." Martha tells Daniel

"Wait a minute, I found this red book in Joseph's house, what does it mean?" asks Daniel as he was handing the book over to Martha.

Martha opened up the book and she skimmed through a few pages in it. "Hmmm, seems Egyptian. I don't read or speak Egyptian. You might have to go to a museum and find someone who can read it and translate it for you." She suggested it to Daniel.

"Fuck, I know who to call and who can do it." Benson tells Martha as she was handing the book back to him.

"Who?" She asks,

"My Irish ex father-in-law. He has hated me ever since I married his daughter and then cheated on her. He is the head doctor at the New York natural museum. He speaks Egyptian and knows what it means but also French, Spanish, and Chinese. He is a tough old bastard. Oh boy, he will enjoy seeing my ass again." Benson tells Martha.

As Benson was putting the book in the pocket, he had a worried look on his face for Martha. "Listen I don't know if you have family or not but get out of town, go somewhere where they can't find you. Whatever they are just packed up some stuff and go just come with me back to New York" he tells her.

"I wish I could, but I have to take care of Ronda here. She needs me, and I would love to go but this is where I belong. I'm sorry, okay, but I'm also sorry for making you sleep with me. But thank you for saving me with Joseph" she tells Benson. As Martha got close to Daniel, she gave him a kiss on the cheek and got close to his ear and whispered something in his ear. "Be safe and don't get killed." she tells him after they got done hugging, he just smiled at her, and he left the building.

When Daniel left, Ronda came back out. "Does he know?" she asks Martha.

"No, he doesn't. I didn't tell him." Martha tells Ronda.

"Get everything ready. The Invictus Society must know about him. We have two days." Ronda warned Martha.

"Yes, mother. Should I make the call to the Invictus Society to let them know the one is here?" Martha asks her mom.

"Do it." Ronda tells Martha.

"Yes mother." she says as she went to the back to make a phone call to let the Invictus Society know that the one they have prophet for years, is here.

Chapter Nine

Back at the hotel Daniel was packing up all of his things to head to the train station to head back to New York to see his ex-father-in-law. As Daniel was getting everything ready, he still had the red book that he found at Joseph's house, he opened a page on it, and he just stared and looked at the pictures. "Fuck, you better help me you old Irish bastard." Benson tells himself. There was a knock on Daniels' hotel room door. Benson looked confused wondering who it was as he was walking towards the door and checked the peep hole to see who it was. As he got close and looked at the peep hole it was Shepard.

Daniel looked shocked in horror thinking to himself. "How in the hell did he find me?"

Shepard kept knocking on his door, getting louder. "DETECTIVE DANIEL BENSON! I KNOW YOU ARE IN THERE! COME OUT WITH YOUR HANDS UP! YOU ARE UNDER ARREST FOR THE MURDER OF ONE JOSEPH O'MALLEY!"

Benson opened the window to his hotel and when he looked down, he knew he was screwed. They were five stories down. Either he can break his legs or get killed. Shepard was kicking down the door now as Daniel kept looking at the door and at the window. Daniel kept seeing what he could land on, the sidewalk, then the door. As Benson went to get his bag and his dad's lucky hat. He threw his bag out of the window, and he started to put his body out of the window. The door finally broke and Shepard and a few police officers came rushing in to see Benson go out the window. Daniel threw his body out of the window he closed his eyes and started praying to God to land somewhere soft or something to break his fall.

CRASH

As luck would have it, Benson landed on some trash cans and lids and a lot of trash. "I guess I didn't see that. holy hell!" says Benson.

As Shepard and the rest of the police officers looked down at Daniel, they were shocked he survived. "I'M DOWN HERE YOU BIG HORSES ASS!" Daniel tells Shepard. As Daniel was getting up, he tried to get his bag then he felt a sharp pain in his thigh. He looks over to see a big broken glass bottle stuck in his thigh.

"FREEZE!" Shepard yells at Daniel as he and the rest of the police officers were leaving.

There was no time to waste. Benson had no choice but to get the glass out of his side and move. As he took the glass out of his side, blood squirted out and he started to bleed. Benson got his bag and tried to run but couldn't. The more he ran the more blood came out, leaving trails of blood for Shepard to find him. Benson limped to an alley to hide out he found some doors, but they were all locked "Fuck!" exclaims Daniel. He had nowhere else to go. He then heard a gun hammer click behind his head.

"Don't move Benson!" It was Shepard's voice. "Turn around very slowly." As Benson was turning around slowly, he was Shepard's form again.

"What the fuck are you?" Daniel asks Shepard. Before Shepard could say anything, Daniel spoke again. "Because you look like a damn shaved bird with sharp teeth and pointy ears," says Daniel.

"You got jokes, I'll give you that." Shepard hissed at Daniel. "I can finally tell my goddess, my queen, that I got the great Daniel Benson, and I can tell her that I killed him. We will be gone from this curse for good." says Shepard. "Any last words for the late great Benson?" Shepard asks him.

As Daniel looked at Shepard, he saw who was behind Shepard and he grinned. "Yeah, fuck you!"

Then all of a sudden, a long sword or knife came out of Shepard's chest killing him instantly. As Shepard's body dropped on the ground it was Martha who was holding a big sword of some sort, then Benson looked at his wound. The pain to his thigh was getting to him and he was losing blood.

"Are you okay?" Martha asks Daniel.

"I'm fine." Daniel looked at Shepard's dead body. "He's not." Then he fell to the ground.

As Daniel came too, he was at Martha's apartment. "Wa...what happened?" Daniel asks Martha.

"You got hurt so I took you into my place to fix you up." she tells Daniel.

As Daniel was getting out of her bed, he saw the bandage on his thigh, and it was nice and clean. "Thanks Martha but what is going on? First, I saw your boss turn into one ugly motherfucker, then I saw Shepard do the same thing, but

Shepard was different. He looked like my ex high school girlfriend Nancy when she didn't have her makeup on and she's ugly." Daniel jokingly tells Martha.

"Alright I might as well tell you, but you won't believe it when I tell you. Do you want some coffee?" she asks.

"Yes, with sugar cubs please." he says as they both got their coffee and they both sat down

"Okay here it goes."

Chapter Ten

"I don't know if you believe in voodoo or vampires, but since then, New Orleans has been weird. Since something arrived when I killed Shepard, he was a vampire. Ronda is not my friend. She is my mom. She is a high witch. She has been alive for almost two hundred years, and she keeps saying the prophet one is coming and he too will be immortalized."

Daniel looked up thinking Martha was a crazy person. he looked at his coffee and after he drank all of it, he put his cup down on the table and says, "Okay, I don't believe what you are saying because there is no such things as vampires or demons, or evil witches, or werewolves, if Joseph, Shepard and Jennifer were vampires then how come Shepard didn't burn in the sun like Joseph and Jennifer did?" Benson questioned Martha.

"Because whoever he was talking about made him walk in the sunlight. Joseph and Jennifer, they were just begging to turn. They needed more blood and more victims. Whoever knows you didn't like your exes from what I saw with Jane and with you with Jennifer. we are working on it." she tells Daniel.

"Well, you can believe it all you want. I don't believe a goddamn thing and right now I don't trust anyone right now. But as of right now, I want to get on that train and go back to New York and find out what the hell is in this red book that

I found in Joseph's house now if you..." Daniel stopped and he had to sit back down as he was getting those headaches again. "Ow my head! Shit this one is bad." Daniel says. "I can't see what the hell is going on with me. I need some whiskey in a hurry." he tells Martha.

As soon as he told Martha that, she hurried to the store to get him some whisky. Benson passed out from the pain again and he began having his dreams again. This time in his dreams he was in it, and he looked like he was in the future New York. He was chasing a female. Benson was wearing all black and had a future weapon with him in his right hand. When the female stops, he asks her to turn around very slowly and put her hands up behind her head. She did what she was told. As she turned around, she looked like a vampire with sharp teeth and glowing red eyes. She was talking, but Daniel couldn't understand what she was saying. Then all of a sudden, she got close to him fast and quick, and she was gonna bite him. Before anything could happen, Martha woke Daniel up. As soon Martha woke up Benson, he got up quick and with a cold sweat he got out his gun being all freaked out and paranoid.

"CALM DOWN DANIEL! IT'S ME MARTHA!"

Daniel, still shaken from what happened, finally put his gun down. "Give me my whisky please." He put his hand out to receive it from Martha. Martha handed him the whisky to put on his hand. As soon as he had it, he opened it and just started chugging it out of the bottle. "Ah good ol jack." says Daniel as Daniel was gonna take another drink of whisky Martha tells Daniel

"What was that all about? you didn't see normal at all you acted like a crazy bird?" Martha questioned him

"You wouldn't understand. I have had these nightmares and headaches since I was twelve years old. I tried everything to get rid of them but as soon as I hit adulthood. I started drinking the good ol Jack Daniels and they stopped." says Daniel. "When my dad went missing when I was two years old, during a case, they only found his gun and his hat. I still have them, as you can tell, but anyway when my dad went missing the nightmares and headaches got worse and now, they are getting worse. I'm scared of what is gonna happen to me in the next few days from your old friend there." Daniel tells Martha.

"Oh my god I'm so sorry. Is there anything I can do for you?" she asks him.

"Yeah, you can as a matter of fact, can you find out what your mom means that I got two days, and also can you find out why or who this Queen, mother, goddess is that Shepard was talking about?" Daniel asks Martha. He was wiping sweat off his face and neck and was walking to get his bag and to get ready to leave for the train station. He had to go back to New York. As he was leaving, Martha stopped him to give him a hug on the way out. She knows what he is and it's killing her because she can't tell Benson what he is or what he is becoming.

"I'll do what I can over here. I will call you or send you a telegram." Martha tells him as they both hug, they both look into each other's eyes. They knew they wanted to have sex again but after what is going on, now is not the time.

"Goodbye Martha," Daniel says to Martha.

She just smiled at him as he was closing the door. Martha started to cry because she knew how it's going to go with Benson. then she heard a noise from the bathroom so she stop crying wipe her tears and went to the bathroom she opened the bathroom door and nothing she look confused as she thought she heard a noise from the bathroom she check behind the shower curtain then she heard another nose again as Martha left the bathroom she was checking under the bed nothing in the closets nothing still looking confused she just says the hell with it and decided to leave the room before she hears more noise. As soon as she opened the door, she had a look of horror and shock on her face.

"NO! NOT YOU! IT CAN'T BE IT'S YOU! AK..."

Someone or something covered her mouth.

Chapter Eleven

As soon as Daniel got to the train station, he went to the bus information office to try to see if he could get a train ticket to New York. As luck would have it, the last train leaves in about thirty minutes. As soon as Benson got his ticket, he found a bench to sit down on. "I have had it in this muggy hot ass town." Benson says even though it was October, New Orleans was still hot and muggy. Benson took another drink of his whisky to keep the headaches away. He just wants to get on the train to sleep it off without any nightmares. He wants to go back home to see his daughter and his ex-wife and hug them and kiss them.

Thirty minutes later, the train that was heading to New York arrived and he was boarding the train to find his seat. Benson thought he saw something out of the corner of his eye. He thought he saw Lady Beneviento holding Martha behind her arms and Beneviento was waving at him. He had to do a double take and he realized they weren't there. Only normal people waving at their loved ones. "I think I better lay down and get some sleep." He says. "But first I need food. I haven't eaten since I got to New Orleans a few days ago. I think it was when me and Martha did it. That was two days ago." Daniel starts digging in his pocket to get his pocket watch. After retrieving it, he checks the time. It was six p.m. "I wonder if the car bar is open?" He says. He looked at his pocket watch and admired it for a minute. Benson then turned it over and looked at the engraving. "We love you" was on the back. Daniel smiled a bit because he got this pocket watch from Rebecca and his unborn baby when he joined the NYPD.

When he finally got some food and drank his whisky, as always as he was dreaming, he thought his nightmares were over and done with when he gets blackout drunk. They came back bad this time, and this time his nightmares were about him, his wife, and his daughter. He saw them tied up trying to warm him. But once he turned around it was too late a hand grabbed him by the neck and tossed him onto the brick wall from what he saw was he look like he was in an old abandoned building and he saw a figure who he couldn't make out the mysterious figure but somehow the figure was able to push the brick walls down on him killing him then when Benson woke up he was in a cold sweat. "What the hell even good ol jack didn't help me what the fuck" he says as he was looking at the empty bottle when the train conductor came by Daniel asking for his ticket so the conductor can punch it. He notices the tattoo on the hand of the conductor, the same one he saw on Joseph and Shepard.

"Excuse me? How long till we reach New York?" Benson asks.

"In about an hour or so." the conductor replies.

"Thank you." Benson tells him.

The conductor left. Benson's face went from worried to shocked. He had to think of a plan. He knew how to get the conductor's attention. Benson took off his brown trench coat and his dad's lucky hat and went in the direction the conductor went. Once he saw the conductor, Benson followed him all the way to the front of the train. When the conductor saw Benson, he walked up to him.

"Can I help you with something sir?" he asks Benson.

"Yes, I'm having a hard time looking for the bathrooms. Can you show me where they are?"

The conductor, who had a confused look on his face, looked at Benson. Daniel went into the conductor's ear.

"I know what the fuck you are. If you wanna live, you go to the bathroom now. I will follow you. Don't try anything stupid or I will toss your ass outside and the train will do its work. Do you understand?" he tells the conductor. The conductor just nodded and went to the bathroom. "The back bathroom." Benson says as they kept walking. Some people were looking up at them, while some other people were just minding their own business.

Once they reached the back bathroom Benson, who still had his gun in his holster, took it out and told the conductor to get inside. Benson went inside too. Once they went inside the small crapped up bathroom Benson says, "I won't kill you if you just answer these questions for me, I might let you live if you become an asshole, I'll toss you out this window capeesh?" The conductor just nodded yes.

"Okay, first of all, I know I keep seeing that tattoo. What the fuck are you guys? Who are you all?" he asks the conductor.

"We are followers, we are minions to our queen, our mother, our goddess." he tells Benson.

"Yeah, yeah, yeah. I keep hearing that about the queen mother, who is she?" asks Benson.

The conductor didn't say anything, just a grin. Benson pointed his gun at him and asked the same question and again the conductor didn't say anything.

"Well looks like we will have to do this the hard way then." Benson says. he pointed his gun at the conductor

"Stupid fool! Your damn weapons won't hurt us and soon our queen will rise to take over this filthy world to cleanse out the filthy humans to make the world better again" he tells Benson.

"Well, you talk, let me guess you are a vampire, and this is your human form? well I can change that." Benson tells him. He tells the conductor, "Turn around and put your hands behind your back." Benson tells him he did what he was told, and they both walked out of the bathroom.

When he opened the door there was a line for the bathroom. "Sorry folks, I caught this guy getting into people's bags and sniffing women's undergarments and men's undergarments as well." Benson tells everyone. The conductor, who had a shocking look on his face started to shake his head no. Before he could reply, Benson says to him, "Move! You sick pervert, good thing I caught you before you were gonna sniff men's feet or sniff their dicks."

They went to the back of the train where there was some rope. Benson tied the rope around the waist of the conductor, he uncuffed him and told him to go over the railing of the train. "Now, I'm gonna ask you again. Who is the queen?" Benson asks him. While Benson is holding his gun and the conductor's hands. Then Daniel noticed the sun was coming up. "Oh, shit you better answer me. The sun is almost up, and I know what happens with you ugly son of a bitches." Benson tells the conductor.

"Okay, okay, okay, I'll tell you just pull me after so I can hide from the sun?" he tells Benson.

"Deal! Spill it out fuckwad." Benson tells him.

"Okay, her name is Akasha. She is our mother, our great mother. She is a great Egyptian queen who has been awake for thousands of years and on Halloween, she will rule the world. Now please help me. I have told you everything." The conductor demands Benson.

"What does she look like?" Benson asks.

"Help me and I will tell you. Please help me, you stupid human!" the conductor tells Benson. Daniel took out his cuff and he cuffed one of the wrist of the conductor and the other side of the cuff at the of the rail of the train.

"WHAT? YOU PROMISED ME YOU WAS GONNA LET ME GO!" the conductor shouted at Benson as the sun began to slowly rise.

As Benson was leaving, he tells him, "No, you stay here and get some vitamin d. It's not like it's gonna kill you." As Benson opened the train door, the sun came out and the conductor's body started to burn.

Chapter Twelve

Once Daniel opened the train door, a little boy came running up to him. The little boy says, "Excuse me sir but what happened to that conductor who was in our bag?" he tells Benson.

Daniel just smiled at him and went to knees to meet the boy eye to eye. "He just left, he was a hothead, so he just left the train, and he was fired." he tells the little boy.

"Oh, okay thank you for keeping us safe." The little boy tells Benson.

As soon as the little boy left, Benson went back outside and there was nothing left. Just the hand of the conductor still cuffed to the railing of the train. "I bet that was his strong hand." Daniel jokingly says. He got the hand and tossed it away. He got his cuffs and uncuffed them and he put them back in his pocket. He was almost to New York, so Benson went back inside to try to rest for a bit.

About thirty minutes later the train finally stopped at New York train station. Benson was getting a bit worried now because he didn't know if he was still a wanted man here in the city. As he got his bag, he walked down the stairs onto the floor. Once Benson hit the doors to the outside. It was cold and raining still in October morning. As the leaves were still falling down, Daniel had admired the view and cold like he had been for the last thirty-five years. But there was no time to waste. He must see his ex-father-in-law at the museum. Benson waved his arm to stop for a cab and one did. Once he got in the cab, he told the driver to head for the museum. A few minutes later he arrived at the Natural History Museum of New York. He got out of the taxi after paying the driver.

"Okay pops, let's see if you don't hit me." Benson tells himself with his bag in his hand. He started climbing up the stairs for the museum. Once Benson got to the doors, he opened it and of course being a workday, it was busy. Benson knew what room number his father-in-law was in. "Okay, here we go." Daniel fixed his hat, and he went walking to find the room his father-in-law was in. When Benson found his office, he had to wait for a minute and collect his thoughts. He took one last good puff of his cigarette and he knocked on his father-in-law's door. He saw a shadow figure coming in the glass door window that says Dr. Quinn O' Connor.

"Oh, is this me daughter and granddaugh..." he starts to say as he opens the door. He saw that it was Benson alone.

"Hi dad."

PUNCH

Benson went down like a sack of potatoes. "Geez pop, you may be an old Irish bastard, but you can still throw a punch." Benson tells him.

"You got some nerve coming here after what you did to me daughter and granddaughter." he tells Benson with his thick Irish accent. "I should kick your arse more." Quinn tells Daniel. "I know Quinn, but you can kick me arse later. I need your help." says Daniel.

"Why should I help you after what you did? You cheated on me daughter." Quinn says.

Quinn O' Connor who was born in Belfast Northern Ireland but came to the states as a little boy, grew up in a poor neighborhood. By the time he was a teenage adult, he lost both of his parents to a sickness. He had to fend for himself, so he kept up with school and went to college. Met his wife and got his doctorate in history. He can speak and write Egyptian, Russian, French, and Chinese. He and his wife only had one child together, Rebecca. Two years ago, he lost his wife to cancer, so he spends most of his time at the museum.

"I'm making it up to her and Leah, but right now like I said, I need your help, Quinn." Benson tells Quinn.

"And why should I help you? You are a cheating bastard?" Quinn asks Daniel.

"Because your daughter and grandchild may be in danger." he tells Quinn "Look I found this book. I don't know what it means but I have been almost shot and killed and arrested for this damn thing. The only thing I know is it's Egyptian writing." Benson tells him. They both looked at each other. Daniel says, "look I don't have time left. Something is gonna happen to me in the next few days and it's what, October twenty ninth? I got a few days left; I could die. I'm trying to fix everything right with Rebecca and Leah. Please dad." Benson was holding up the book.

Quinn took the book from Benson's hands. "I'll do it, but for only me daughter and granddaughter, not for you. I will still want to kick your arse, but I'll do it. Come see me tomorrow morning if you are still alive."

"Thanks dad." Daniel tells Quinn.

Daniel turned around to leave until he heard Quinn say something. "By the way, if you go to church still, now is the time and pray for Rebecca and Leah and for your soul"

Daniel just shook his head and went ahead to leave his office.

He had to see Rebecca and Leah, so he decided to go back to Rebecca's house. Benson hailed a cab, and he went to the house. Once he got there, he went to the front door and knocked. Daniel was feeling really fatigued and was starting to lose energy.

As soon as Rebecca opened the door, she greeted him with a hug. "What are you doing here?" she asks him with her Irish accent.

"I came and saw...I saw uh." Daniel falls on the floor from being exhausted.

Chapter Thirteen

When Daniel came to a few hours later, he was on the couch while Rebecca was on the chair sleeping and watching over him. "Becky?" Daniel says to her as his voice was all horsy and groggy.

"Oh my God, are you okay? You just fell over like a sack of potatoes." she tells him.

"I don't know what happened. From being exhausted or from your father hitting me. I don't know. I'm feeling weird." he tells her.

"Was it the nightmares again?" she asks Benson.

"No, it is something else. I just don't know, but what time is it?" Benson asks Rebecca

"It is nine at night." Rebecca tells Daniel.

"Jesus Christ! I was out for thirteen hours." he says.

"I made you dinner and Leah wanted to see you." Becky tells Daniel.

"I'll go see Leah and get cleaned up." Daniel tells Rebecca. As Daniel was walking up to the bedroom to Leah's room. Once he got to Leah's room, he opened her door gently and she was sound asleep with the stuffed toy he got her. He walked into her room to tuck her in and kiss her forehead.

"Goodnight baby. I promise I will make everything right with your mom and I." he says, then he heard a noise downstairs. "Must be Rebecca getting my dinner out of the oven," he says. He was leaving Leah's room again and took one final look at her before he closed the door. As he was going down the stairs, he noticed some things were knocked over in the front room. He even noticed how the pictures of him, and Rebecca and Leah were broken. "That's weird." he says. Then he heard more noise coming from the kitchen. Once he opened the kitchen door, he saw Rebecca then BAM! Benson was out cold.

Once Benson had awakened again, it was six a.m. He got up from the kitchen floor, and he noticed blood. It wasn't his blood so it must have been from Rebecca. Daniel, who had a shocking and worried look on his face, raced upstairs to see if Rebecca and Leah were in the bedrooms. He checked Leah's room. Gone. He checks Becky's room. Gone. They have been kidnapped. He hurried back downstairs to call the police officers, but then he remembered he was wanted for murder.

"SHIT!" he says. "I have to go back to my office and think of a plan." He can call Quinn and tell him what happened. "I'll call his house phone, if not, then his office phone. He has to be up at this hour." Daniel says. He calls his home phone first.

RING

RING

RING

RING

RING

"What the hell? He usually picks up on the fourth ring. let me try his office phone."

RING

RING

RING

RING

Finally, the phone got picked up.

"Hello? This is Dr. Quinn O' Connor." Quinn says on the other line.

"Dad! Oh my God! I need your help!" Benson tells Quinn.

"What's the matter now? do I have to kick your arse again?" Quinn says to Daniel.

"No! Rebecca and Leah, they have been kidnapped. I can't call the cops, I'm wanted for murder. I don't know what happened, all I know is I saw Rebecca in the kitchen and me being knocked out again," Benson nervously tells Quinn.

Quinn kept quiet for a minute. "You are one stupid bastard. I'll call the cops for you and let them know what happened. Then you come to my office to settle this. I know what the book is all about and what is going on. And when this is all over, I'm gonna kick your arse and then we are gonna drink some Irish whiskey like real men." Quinn angrily tells Benson with that Irish accent.

"I will see you soon dad." he tells Quinn.

"And don't call me that! You have to earn that title with me again. Do what you have to do. I'll see you soon Daniel." he tells Daniel.

When Daniel hung up the phone, he went back upstairs to the master bedroom. Once there, he went to the closet and found his secret stash of weapons. He went back downstairs, and he saw the picture of his family again. He just stares at it, and then he takes it out of the frame. He put the picture in his pocket, and he left the house. He was headed back to the city of his office. Before Benson left, he found the spare car keys to his car that he gave to Rebecca. Once the car started, he took off into the city, it was a thirty-minute drive.

Chapter Fourteen

Once Daniel got his office he walked up the stairs to open the door he hasn't been in here since Pilar got killed by Clark so he don't know what kind of mess it is once he opened the door papers and desk was all over the place he bend to his knees and found more pictures of his mom and dad of him and his sister then another one with his dad, sister and him when he got back up he saw the phone being off the hook once he put it back on the hook he had a phone dial and he started to call Val.

RING

RING

RING

RING

"Hello?" It was Val.

"Val, Thank God you are alright I just got into town it has been a shit show." he tells her.

"Yeah, no kidding, I have been calling and knocking on your office. The papers say you killed and murdered some police officers and Clark. What the hell brother?" Val tells Daniel.

"That wasn't me. I have been set up ever since I left and went to New Orleans. I have been shot and almost killed and almost arrested. Rebecca and Leah are kidnapped." Benson tells Val. Before Val could say anything else, Daniel interrupted her

"Listen, get out of the city it's not safe just get a bag and just get out as far as you can." he told her, and she paused for a minute. "Okay brother you're the cop I'll do what you say good luck and I love you." Val tells Daniel.

"I love you too Val." he says.

As soon as he hung up, he went and got some fresh clothes. He has not taken a shower for the last two days he is sweaty he shirt is covered in blood and sweat from the back of his neck and he has not shaven he need to clear his head and figure out where Rebecca and Leah are and who has them after he got done cleaning his office and taking a shower and a fresh shave and clean clothes he went to his office and he sat down for a minute to figure out where to start he open up his top drawer and found a unopened bottle of jack and a cigar along with his flask he got out the bottle and was tempted to open it. He opened up the window got the bottle and he tossed it out the window he got up from his chair and started to leave to go to Quinn's job when he went outside it was still gloomy and windy but not rainy which was a good thing for once he got in his car and started to head over to the museum after the twenty minute drive to the museum Benson reached his destination he got out of the car and he notice that it was not busy as it was. Once he went inside the museum, it looked like a hurricane hit it, but Daniel had one of those funny cop feelings, so he took out his gun from his holster and started to make his way towards Quinn's office along the way he saw papers on the floor dead bodies of workers, civilians, and cops. "What the hell! It feels like New Orleans again." He says.

Once he reached Quinn's office his door was cracked open a bit, he noticed some blood on the floor, he figured it might be too late, he didn't reach Quinn in time. Daniel opened the door to Quinn's office and his office was a mess of papers on the ground, chairs all over the place, blood on the floor and wall.

"QUINN YOU IN HERE!" Benson yells. "QUINN!" Daniel yells again with his gun out he heard noise coming from the closet Benson slowly walked to the closet and when he opened the door it was Quinn he was hurt and bleeding out his intestines where showing and as a joke someone took his other intestines and acted like they was choking Quinn with them like a rope Benson went down on one knee to check on Quinn. "Oh my god Quinn what the hell happened?" Daniel says to Quinn.

"You took your sweet arse time getting here all hell broke loose." Quinn tells Daniel as Quinn was holding in his stomach to make sure nothing else falls apart.

"Hang in there you tough out Irish bastard I'm gonna get the ambulance they will save you." Benson tells him.

As Benson was gonna get up to get the phone Quinn grabbed him by the wrist to pull him back down. "Laddy, it's too late for me, you have time to save me daughter and granddaughter" says Quinn.

"I can't do this without you Quinn. I don't know who did this to you." Benson tells Quinn.

"Son, all you need to know is in my top desk drawer, it's locked." Quinn says to Daniel as Quinn was reaching in his pocket to get the keys to give out to Daniel. Once he got the keys, he handed them over to Benson. "I... I love you son. Now get your wife and child and kill that bitch!" Quinn says to Daniel.

As Quinn took his last breath Daniel had tears coming out and rolling down his face. As he looked at Quinn for the last time as he was closing Quinn's eyes. he tells Quinn. "I love you too dad. I'm gonna get our family back. I promise."

Once he got up from his knee, his pant leg was covered in blood, but he didn't have time to change. He went to Quinn's top locked drawer and with the key, he opened it. He found notes and the meaning and interrupted what the red book says and from the transfers it says, "To the queen goddess, our Egypt queen, our great mother Akasha. Every thousand years you come out of your tomb, and you feed and get rid of the leeches, and you cleanse the world of filth. To us, your minions, we thank you and for the next one thousand years we shall rule the world with our great mother and the rest of the six gods of vampires Mikael, Finn, Elijah, Klaus, Kol, and Rebekah, our six gods and our great mother Akasha we will have a new world." Benson turned it over to the other page. "We have killed all of the hunters that have hurt us and killed us. Our time is now. First the place called the United States, then the world. We will kill and cleanse the whole world." After that Benson dropped the letters and he noticed a drawing of what looks like the great mother Akasha. "WHAT THE FUCK!" Daniel says as his face was all shocked. The picture of Akasha looked like his client Lady Deedra Beneviento. Benson dropped the picture to the floor as he was angry and now more pissed off as it was just a plan to get Benson set up and wanted him to be set up for murder and God knows whatever plans she had for him then Quinn's phone rang.

RING

RING

RING

RI...

"Hello?" Daniel says to whoever was on the line.

"You missed your last few appointments sir." the female says to Benson.

"PILAR! I thought you were dead." Benson says to her.

"I was, then your client made me an offer I couldn't refuse, so I took it," says Pilar.

"Where are my wife and daughter?" Daniel angrily asks Pilar.

"Don't worry about them. The great mother is preparing them for the celebration for all hallows eve. She asked me to call you and to let you know that you are invited, and we have got more guests coming, so don't be late. The party won't start without you. At eleven p.m. sharp. At the old, abandoned warehouse on 20th and Queens and come alone." says Pilar.

As the phone click on the other end Daniel was still on the phone now being more pissed off he took the phone and threw it on the wall before leaving Quinn's office he took Quinn's body and laid it down on the floor Benson took his brown trench coat and covered Quinn's body with it before he left Quinn's office he notice something sharp hidden in the closet. From what it looked like it was a golden dagger, and it had a little note with it.

"Quinn, use this when the time is right. When my son knows the truth." Willie Benson. `

"Dad?" called out Daniel as Daniel looked confused with the dagger in his hand, he had no time to leave but first he made a promise to Quinn he was heading to church. Once he got outside the weather was getting worse Benson took out his pocket watch and it almost noon he had eleven hours left so he better do what he needs to do once he got in his car he drove to the church him and Rebecca got married at an old Irish church once Benson was heading to the church there was hardly any traffic well this weather it gets bad but not bad like this. Once he got to the church he got out of his car and Benson was running to the church holding his hat and praying that the door was open "Thank God!" Benson says as a sign of relief. "Hello Father O'Malley?" says Daniel.

A few minutes later the father comes out in his attire with grayish hair holding the bible "Ah me son, how are you? I was about to close shop due to the storm" says Father O'Malley with the Irish accent.

"Not good father, not everything is alright. I lost my family. I need some prayers and advice" Benson tells the father.

"Talk to me son, what is troubling you?" O'Malley says to Benson.

"My family has been kidnapped Quinn; my father-in-law is dead. I'm set up for murder and now for some reason my dad left Quinn a gift saying, "When the time is right." Father, do you believe in the supernatural? Like vampires?" Benson asks the father.

Chapter Fifteen

"Why yes son, I believe in the supernatural like the vampires, demons, and whatever else the devil lays on the ground for us. Why do you ask me son?" Father O'Malley asks Benson.

Daniel was trying to shake off the heading and fatigue. "Father, I think something is wrong with me. I'm not feeling well so I need to leave." Benson tells the father.

Daniel was leaving Father O'Malley says, "GO WITH GOD ME SON!"

Daniel stopped, turned around to look at Father O'Malley and says, "GOD IS GONNA SIT THIS ONE OUT!" Then Benson left the church.

The storm was getting worse now. "I need to see if Val left town." Benson says to himself. he was heading for his sister's bar when the storm was getting way worse he was speeding up to his sister's bar and place about it as well when Daniel got there it was closed the doors was locked but he notice thought the door window look like there has been a scuffle he left the front door and went to the backway once he made his way to the backway of the building Daniel notices the back door was locked too as well. He looked up at the fire escape to go to her window just then he heard a voice behind him.

"FREEZE BENSON DON'T MOVE!" a police officer tells Daniel. "PUT YOUR HANDS BEHIND YOUR HEAD!"

Daniel just shook his head, put his hands up and tells the police officer, "I was fram...OH MY GOD!" When Benson turned around it was one of ugly creatures. "Let me guess you're a vampire and want to suck my blood or take me to see the queen mother Akasha," says Benson. Benson tells the vampire "We'll let me tell you something fugly. You look like something I shit out of every morning. You look like shaved burned balls that got put in the oven. I have had it with you ugly fucks. I'm gonna kill you, kill everyone ya's, kill that bitch Akasha and THERE IS NOTHING YOU CAN DO ABOUT IT!"

Then all of a sudden Daniel lost control of his emotions and attacked the vampire. Then when Daniel came too, he was shocked about what happened. The vampire's body was torn into shreds into pieces. "Fuck me I did that" says Benson Daniel picked up his hat and held on to it and started to climb up the fire escape to get to Val's room and once he reached her window figures it was locked. Benson bend his elbow to break the window just so his hand and arm can unlocked the window once he got inside the apartment building he took out his gun and starting saying his sister's name but she didn't reply he went to her bathroom and nothing as well he put his gun away he went back to the front room and sat on her chair to think where she could of gone. He felt woozy but he had to get up and keep going. Once Daniel got up, he noticed a note on the coffee table, and it just had one word on it. "Prepare." Daniel with a confused look on his trying to think of what she meant by prepare.

"Preparing for what?" he says. He went to Val's bedroom again and went to her closet. "Fuck her clothes and suitcase is still here. I better check downstairs." Benson hurried to the front door to open it and there was a dead body. The dead body wasn't Val, but another vampire-like creature. He bent down to see who it was, and it was just a random person. Benson checks the person's pockets and to see if they had the same tattoo and yes, they do have the same tattoo he saw back in New Orleans. The tattoo is shaped like a cross with an oval. It looked kind of like a cross but different. Then Daniel remembered something about what Quinn was talking about one day, when both of them were getting drunk.

"ANKH!" Benson says all loud and proud. "See you old Irish bastard. I was paying attention, ankh, it means life and immortality in Egyptian." says Benson. As Benson got up, he started to go downstairs to see what kind of mess was at his sister's bar. Once Benson reached the final step of the floor, the bar looked like a storm hit it. Benson checked every chair and table and nothing. No blood, nothing, even behind the bar, no blood, just broken glass and tables and chairs flipped over.

"What the hell happened? Where is Val?" Daniel holstered his gun and picked up a bar stool and just sat down, took off his hat and was just being stressed and frustrated. He turned over to the bar and he saw a picture of him and Val together. Then he took out his wallet and took out his picture of him, Rebecca, and Leah. He grins because he knows what he has to do. Finish the case. He looked at his pocket watch to see what time it was three pm. He had eight hours left and the storm outside was still bad, so he just stayed at the bar till then he went to his shirt pocket and took out a cigar. "Damn I was gonna save this when I finish my case. Might as well smoke it. After he got done smoking his cigar and getting him something to eat at the bar, Daniel's mind was focused and cleared. He is ready to go battle with the undead Daniel is going to get his loved ones back after he checked his pocket watch again, it was ten p.m. He has been at the bar since three Benson is ready to leave but first, he must make a stop at the police station. He made his way back upstairs to Val's apartment. He kicked the dead body for good measure. He went out the window. The storm had stopped once. It was just cold, and the moon was full. Once Daniel landed on the ground he went to his car, and someone was standing next to his car.

"Father O'Malley, what are you doing here?" asks Benson.

"Ah me son, this is where I come to every night. To your sister's bar for food and a pint. When I noticed her doors was closed and your car was here, I thought I went here." O'Malley says.

"Look father, my sister is gone too, someone bored the doors and there is a dead body of what looks like a vampire you have to believe me now please father?" Benson says begging for O'Malley to believe him

"Alright me son, what can I do to help?" he asks Benson. Daniel, taking out a flask from out of his pocket, was shaking it to see if there was any liquor left. There was, he opened the flask up and drained what was left of it. Once it was all gone, he tossed it to the father. "Fill this up with holy water and get all the crosses you can at the church and meet me at 20th and queens at the old abandoned warehouse by midnight." Benson tells O'Malley.

"I me son so we are doing the lord's work." O'Malley tells Benson as he puts the flask away.

"Yes, father and at this point I don't care if I live or die. I'm gonna send these devil's these demon's back to hell and watch your ass father." Daniel tells O'Malley.

O'Malley went to his car and started heading to the church. While Daniel was going to the police station.

Once Daniel reached the police station he had to find a way to get inside without being arrested then he remember the back way to the building so Benson walked all the way to the back of the building but to his surprise the door was gone Clark took down that door and just put a brick wall to cover it up "fucking Clark" says Daniel. "Looks like we're going in guns blazing" he says as he walked back to the front of the police station, he was hoping there may be one or two police officers inside. Once he went inside of the building there were three police officers inside. The desk police officer, the radio police officer and just an extra police officer. Daniel went up to the desk police officer.

"Hello, can you help me?" Benson asks the old police officer.

"Yes, can I help you?" asks the old cop with his froggy voice.

"Yes, I was wondering if I can go through your files for a case, I'm a private detective and I heard the files might be here." Daniel tells the police officer.

Just before the old police officer could answer the other police officer noticed Daniel from the wanted picture.

"Hey pal, don't move." The other police officer tells Benson.

Daniel pulled out his gun at the police officers and the desk police officer froze. "I hate to do this to you, guys but I have no other choice." says Daniel. The police officer nodded and called for the other police officer. Once the other police officer came into the front, he put his hands up. "Good job guys. Now drop your guns and come to the front of the desk." says Daniel. All three police officers were in the front. Okay very good now turn around and cuff one another wrist to wrist." says Benson. The police officers did what they were told to do. "Now give me the keys now and move to the nearest cell." he tells the police officers.

Once the cops all handed out their keys to Daniel, they walked to the nearest jail cell. Once Benson got the jail cell open, he tells them to go inside. Once inside he tells them, "Look, I should be happy with you all because your former captain didn't corrupt you. I promise I won't be long. I just need guns. Once I'm done, just give me a five-minute head start to leave. I didn't kill your boss. Your boss did that to himself." Daniel tells them.

Chapter Sixteen

Once Daniel locked the police officers up, he went to the armory and evidence locker room. That is where he got a lot of weapons: shotguns, pistols, and hell he even found John Dillinger's Tommy gun. Once he got what he was looking for, he loaded up his car and was ready to go. Before he could leave, he had to let the police officers go. Once back inside, he went to the jail cell.

"Okay, I made a promise to you all. Don't try any funny stuff. I left your guns at the front desk. Here are the keys, remember a five-minute head start." Benson tossed the keys inside of the jail cell and he took off running. Once he got inside of his car he headed towards the abandoned warehouse.

Once Daniel got there, Father O'Malley was already there waiting for him.

"Hello Father O'Malley looks like you beat me here. Anything going on or have you seen anything going inside that building?" Benson asks O'Malley.

"No, I can't see a thing. The windows are all covered up, but I hear chanting and I keep hearing two women screaming and a little girl crying for her daddy." says O'Malley.

Daniel says, "Shit, it has to be them. Come on Father. I have gifts in the trunk of the car."

They both went to the back of the car and when Benson opened the trunk, he had nothing but stacks of weapons. "Hope you know how to shoot Father, because it's time to send these damn ugly motherfuckers to hell!" Daniel tells O'Malley. "Take your pick."

As Benson was grabbing the golden dagger and another trench coat along with the shotgun and John Dillinger's Tommy gun, "Is that Dillinger's gun? Where did you get that at?" Father O'Malley asks Benson.

"From a corrupt cop named Clark." answers Benson.

They were loading up the weapons when Daniel checked his pocket watch. He had about fifteen minutes till eleven. "Okay Father, here's the plan. We find a way inside the building, and we go in and see if they have my daughter and wife inside there." Daniel tells O'Malley.

"Wee, I like your plan son, but what if you just go to the front door and I'll just be ready on your signal?" O'Malley suggests Benson with that Irish accent of his.

"That's a good plan too, Father. Let's go with your idea. Hand me that flask with the holy water in it." says Benson.

The father didn't do it as O'Malley left already heading to the building, Benson tells O'Malley, "Father, watch your ass." Father O'Malley nodded his head and grinned then went to the back building while Daniel was gonna make his way to the front building.

As soon as Benson reached the front of the building, he opened the door. He was making his way in. There was nothing but candles lighting up every room. Benson can hear noises coming from not too far away. He locked and loaded the tommy gun, made sure it was ready to be fired upon. As Benson got closer, he could hear people moaning like they were having sex. Once he got close to the room where the noise was coming from, he opened the door and sure enough, Akasha's minions were having a sex orgy. They were having sex in puddles of blood. Benson opened the door wider, and he found Akasha bathing in a pool of blood. He cocked the hammer of the tommy gun and pointed it at Akasha.

"Lady Deedra or should I say, Akasha?" Benson says to her.

Akasha turned around and she covered her breast. "How dare you come in here while I'm having my bathing time. this is not a gentleman like you." she says acting in that southern belle accent.

"Cut the shit bitch! I know you're not from the south. I know who you really are. You said you wanted me here so, here I am. I should shoot you now and be over and done with." says Benson.

Akasha didn't say anything at first. She just got up from her blood bath while several male minions helped her get out. Akasha says, while changing her voice from southern to her real voice. "Very well, if you shoot me, then you will never find your family. In fact, I think someone should show you where they are." she says in her evil sinner Egyptian voice.

Just then, Benson felt a cold hard chamber of a gun against his head. He heard the gun cock, so he turns around to see who it was. His jaw dropped. "Father O' Malley? But why?" asks Daniel.

"You see my boy; it was I who called out the great mother. I got tired of all the sinners, not paying for their sins and not accepting the lord, so, I had to do what I had to do. So, I made a deal with this fine young lady in exchange for your daughter." O'Malley explains to Benson.

"My daughter? But why?" Benson asks him.

"For a new body. You see, Akasha needs a new body and some new young fresh blood. If she doesn't then her body will turn into stone, and she won't be able to rule the world for another thousand years." O'Malley tells Benson.

"So, it was you who planned the whole thing all along? Getting me set up at the train station? Getting me set up in New Orleans, killing Quinn. I should kill you now and send you to hell!" Benson tells him angrily.

"SHUT IT!" O'Malley yells, and he hits Benson on the back of the head.

"Now be a good dear and drop your weapon." Akasha tells Benson. He did what he was told, and they all began to leave.

As Benson was leading the way with his hands up, he kept talking. "I bet you ain't shit without that gun father. No wait, I take it back, you're not a Father for the church. You're a fucking evil old man. which I bet you can't get it up no more." Benson tells O'Malley.

"SHUT IT!" he shouts at Daniel.

"Shit I'm not gonna lie. I was aroused when I saw Akasha naked. I bet you did too, but you couldn't get it up." Benson insulted him again and again, trying to get under the skin of O'Malley. "Hey, O'Malley, how many times have you had sex? I bet it was none. I had sex so many times I lost count. How much time for you? I forgot you're an eighty-year-old virgin." Benson laughs at O'Malley.

"THAT'S IT I'M GONNA SHOOT THIS SINNER FOR HAVING TOO MUCH SEX!" O'Malley yelled at Akasha.

"ENOUGH!" Akasha says, "We are finally here."

Once they reached the double doors, Daniel saw who was tied. Rebecca, Leah, and Martha.

"DADDY!" cried Leah after seeing him. Benson wanted to run but his life and his family's life depended on him.

"It's okay baby daddy's here." he says to Leah. "Becky? Martha? Are you all, okay?" He asks. They both nodded yes as their mouths were tied up as well.

"Stop!" Akasha yells out. "Now turn around!" she demands Daniel.

Chapter Seventeen

"Why did you bring me here? Let them go. it's me you want. let them go, you pale looking ugly bitch." he tells Akasha.

"The reason I brought you here is not only a celebration of my new life and body but for you as well" she continued. "You see Benson, twas I who killed your father and mother. twas I who killed Clark and his goons and yes twas I who killed Quinn. twas I who killed my husband because he knew my secret. Now I must do what is right and kill the last of the goddamn bloodline. too bad your sister is not here. I would have enjoyed eating her skin and bones and shitting out her skull." Akasha tells Daniel. "Now keep looking at your family because this will be the last time you will see them." she tells him.

"But why...why are you doing this?" He asks her.

"You see, back in Uruk, known as Iraq now, at a young age. Before the first pyramid was built, I was married to Enkil, the king of Kemet. which would later become Egypt. My husband and I wanted our subjects to turn away from cannibalism and encouraged them to eat grains by farming. Years later I became a beloved ruler for my people. I made sure they were turned away from violence and toward peace. Then one day I became interested in some magic, and I invited twin witch sisters Maharet and Mekare to commune with the spirits. But they refused their queen, so I retreated back by sending my soldiers to their village. which happens to be at the time to be at their mother's funeral rite of eating their mother's brain and heart. My soldiers killed everyone in that village but spared the twins by arresting them for the crime of cannibalism. Once they were in jail, they summoned a powerful spirit named Amel to seek revenge on me. That spirit punished me, my husband and our bodyguard Khayman night and day, day and night and it drove us mad. One night some cannibals came into our house and stabbed me and my husband. leaving us both mortally wounded. when I left my body, my soul got snatched by Amel and we combined our spirits back in my body making me the first world's first vampire." Akasha tells Benson. "I would tell you more about the story but it's almost time for you to die." she tells Daniel. As Daniel was looking at his family and Martha, he knew what was gonna happen to him. "Before you die Daniel, I want you to see this. I'm gonna let you pick for yourself." Akasha tells Daniel.

She waved some of her minions to hold Daniel down to his knees, so he wouldn't get away. "Pilar, O'Malley hold the little brat." says Akasha. Both of them went and held down Leah so her head and body wouldn't move any further. As Akasha was turning around to get a golden cup, she cut open her hand to pour some of her blood inside of the cup. Once she got the amount of blood, she got inside of the golden cup. Akasha turned right back towards Benson's daughter Leah.

"I'm like Jesus Christ. This is my blood. drink it in memory of me." says Akasha. She went to pour her blood inside of Leah's mouth.

Leah spit it back out. "YOU LITTLE CUNT BITCH!"

SMACK!

Akasha smacked Leah on the side of the face. Rebecca couldn't do anything, just looked in horror and shock. Daniel tried to get up, but the minion vampires were strong at holding him down. He had a pissed off face.

"NOW! let's try this again and this time you drink it and swallow it. Pilar, you hold her nose and mouth so she can swallow." she says. This time Akasha poured the blood inside of Leah's mouth. As soon as she did Pilar covered her mouth and her nose to make sure Leah swallowed Akasha's blood. As soon as Leah did, O'Malley and Pilar let go of Leah.

"Let him go." Akasha tells her minions.

They let Daniel go and he went straight for Leah. He picked up Leah's body trying to wake her. "BABY! BABY! WAKE UP! PLEASE! IT'S YOUR DADDY! WAKE UP!" Benson yells at Leah. She was still in her long pink pajamas, and her hair in pigtails.

"BRING ME THE SWORD O'MALLEY!" Akasha tells him. O'Malley ran to the back to get the sword. "MY PEOPLE! IT WAS A SUCCESS! SOON I WILL BE OUT OF THIS BODY AND BE IN A NEW ONE ON ALL HALLOWS EVE!" Akasha yelled at her people.

A few minutes later O'Malley came back with the sword. "Here you go, great mother." he tells her as he was handing off the sword to Akasha.

Meanwhile Benson was rocking Leah back and forth trying to wake her up.

"You stupid mortal fool. she won't wake up until the transfer is complete, but you can stop it." Akasha tells Benson. "You have two choices. One, you can kill your daughter, and the spell

transfer is over and done or two, you can kill yourself and she will go back to herself, and I will die." she tells Daniel as she dropped the sword at him. He was still holding Leah, kissing her forehead. Benson put her back down on the ground and he picked up the sword. He looked at Rebecca and Martha. Rebecca started to cry while Martha just nodded yes to him. "DO IT! DO IT! DO IT! DO IT NNNNNOOOOWWWWWWWWWWWWW!" Akasha yells at Benson. "IIIIIIIIIIIIIIIIIIIIIIII."
STAB.

Chapter Eighteen

Daniel didn't stab Leah; he didn't stab himself. He stabbed Akasha. Once Akasha saw what Benson did to her. She got mad.

"YOU STUPID LITTLE MAN! NOW YOU MUST PAY!" she tells Benson as she was taking the sword out of her stomach. As soon as she took the sword out, she got Benson by the face and lifted him off the ground and just started to slam him on the floor multiple times. She threw him on the wall. Once his whole body hit a wall and he landed on the floor and with her powers she managed to get the wall full of bricks onto Benson. Once Akasha got done with Daniel, she says, "Time to celebrate and continue with the ceremony." Akasha tells everyone. "Bring the girl to the ceremony table so we can continue with the ritual." she says.

"What about Daniel?" O'Malley asks Akasha.

"He's dead, but you want to double check, be my guest and if he has any good things take it." Akasha says to O'Malley.

Akasha and the rest of her followers went to the other room, taking Rebecca and Martha along as well.

Meanwhile Daniel was unconscious and was having his dreams again, but this time it was a good dream. He was in a dark place. He was hearing voices left and right. Then all of a sudden, he saw some glowing eyes coming towards him and with a snap of some fingers a glowing light came on. And it was his mom and dad.

"Hello son it's good to see you. you look great." Benson's mom says to him.

"Mom? Dad? Oh my god! I have never been so happy to see you. But I'm dead and this is heaven?" Benson asks his folks.

"No Daniel, this is in your dream right now, but now is the time to tell you the secret we have been hiding from you since you were a child." his dad tells Daniel. "You see your mom was a slave, a vampire, a minion to Akasha, but she got tired of her killing ways. Akasha tells her followers that if they leave, she will find them and kill them one by one." Benson's dad continued. "When she had the chance, she left Egypt and came to the states to New York to find a better life. We met and fell in love, got married and had you and your sister." his dad tells Daniel.

"So do you mean to tell me that I'm a half vampire?" Benson questioned his parents.

"Yes, honey you are a half vampire, but we call them dhampirs." his mom answered.

Benson's question, "So is Val a vampire or a dhampir as well?" he says.

"No, it is rare that a female vampire and a male human have half vampires. we were hoping it was gonna skip you." Daniel's mom explains.

"So, what now? Do I eat people now? Kill them suck on their blood?" Benson questions his mom and dad.

His mom says, "No baby you are still human which means you have all the powers of a vampire but the good side. This is your gift. Akasha killed me when you were just a month old. your daddy and sister did a good job raising you and you followed in your father's footsteps." his mom says to Benson.

"Daniel, remember when I told you I got a hot tip at the warehouse that was for Akasha. I wanted justice for your mom and us, but I didn't make it before she killed me. She told me she was gonna find you and your sister to end the bloodline." Daniel's dad tells him.

"So, when will I get these powers, are they in effect right now because it's Halloween?" he asks them.

"Yes, honey you just need to let your anger out, you will have the power and strength." his mom tells him.

"Hey, look son, you can use your powers on this asshole." Benson's dad was pointing at O'Malley.

"Go son. We love you. This is your gift, use it for good." his mom says.

Daniel hugged both of his parents.

"Oh, and son, KILL THE MEGA BITCH!" says Daniel's dad.

"One more question dad" Daniel says to his dad

"What's that son?" his dad said

"Did Quinn know about the bloodline and about mom?" he said

"Yes, he did he hid the dagger till you were ready if you use that dagger on the mega bitch she will die" his dad said.

Benson just smiled and nodded as he was about to come to as O'Malley was moving the bricks out of Daniel's body to see what he could have in Benson's pockets. The bricks moved fast exposing Daniel's arm he grabbed father's O'Malley's arm, and he ripped out of his socket Benson got up moving the bricks off of him his body was different he looked younger he had fangs coming out and his eyes were glowing red, and he drank some blood coming out of O'Malley's arm. O'Malley, who was still on the ground holding his stump trying not to bleed out, had a look of horror on his face. As Daniel was coming towards him O'Malley who was just frozen with fear couldn't get up. As Benson got closer to him, he picked him up from his collar and put him back on his feet. They locked eyes then Benson cleaned up the father's collar and straightened out the father's hair. After he did that, he went to the father's ear and said, "BOO!" O'Malley, frozen with fear, just took off to the other room. As Benson was looking at his new body and powers, he was digging through the rubble to look for his dad's lucky hat. After some digging, he found it and he started to go to the other room where the ceremony was taking place.

Meanwhile in the other room, Akasha was doing the rituals with her followers. She was about to stab Leah in the chest to complete the rituals with Rebecca and Martha looking.

"Don't be sad Rebecca or should I say mom you will have new daughter soon" Akasha says to Rebecca

"Once you do that, I'll kill ya myself!" Rebecca says to Akasha.

"Funny, your father said the same thing before I killed him and ripped out his intestines. Then I used them as rope to choke him." Akasha says to her. Rebecca went from mad to sad. When Akasha was about to finish up the ritual, the doors burst open, and it was Father O'Malley.

"Help me! Help me! He is right behind me!" O'Malley yelled as he was closing the doors and holding them shut.

"Who's behind you?" asks Pilar.

"Daniel! He is right behind me!" he says.

"Nonsense. I killed him, you're talking foolishly." Akasha tells O'Malley.

"It's true, he ripped out my arm and I'm losing more blood. We gotta get him...." As soon as O'Malley was talking. The door swung open hard, knocking over the father on the floor hard. Everyone turned around and it was Benson with red glowing eyes and fangs and holding the sword.

Chapter Nineteen

"HEY MEGA BITCH! LET'S DANCE!" Benson says to Akasha while he was pointing the sword out to her.

She pointed her finger back at him and told her followers. "GET HIM AND KILL HIM!"

They all got together and started to run towards Benson.

"Okay, let's see if these powers work." he tells himself. With the sword, he started killing the followers one at a time. Some of the followers had to stay back to protect the great mother and make sure Rebecca and Martha wouldn't do anything.

As the fighting was going on Akasha took Leah and went upstairs. She tells one of her followers to kill Rebecca and the witch bitch. As Benson was slicing and dicing his way to the front of the girls, he saw Akasha taking Leah up the stairs. Being pissed off even more, he went to the ground with the sword and did a very powerful three sixty. After Benson did that, he saw one of the followers about to kill Rebecca, so he threw the sword with all his might and stabbed him in the chest. Then Daniel ran as fast as he could to punch out the heart of the other follower that was also headed towards Rebecca. Benson was a bloody mess from the battle. He had fallen to the ground, out of breath. He needed a minute to breathe. He turned over to see Rebecca and Martha. He crawled to them.

"Don't be scared. I'm not like that bitch." he tells Rebecca as he was untying her. Go untie Martha and head up I gotta deal with one more person" he says to her

"Wha...what are you, Daniel?" she asks him.

"I'll explain later. Now GO!" He tells Rebecca.

Rebecca started to untie Martha like she was told. Daniel began to make his way towards Father O'Malley, who was still on the ground bleeding like a stuffed pig. Once Benson got close with the father, he bent down and spoke.

"Your vision didn't work out for you. Now look, you are bleeding out with a stumpy arm." he tells the father.

"I'm a man of God. I can do lots of things. This was going to be one of them. I'm a man of many things." he tells Benson.

"Oh yeah, clap," Benson insulted him.

Benson got up with the sword in his hand still, he started to push the sword down to his heart. "Father, before I put the sword further down to kill you, I'm letting you know now, you won't be going to heaven. You will be going to hell." Benson tells him.

"I could give a shit! Fuck you! I'll see you down there." O'Malley tells Daniel.

When Daniel pushed the sword down to his heart he said, "Ashes to ashes and dust to dust." Once the father was dead, Benson took the sword out and he was about to head upstairs when he smelled someone he knew.

"Pilar, this is not your fight. I know you are behind me, but this is not your fight." he said as he turned around and he saw that she was holding a dagger.

"You don't understand. I have to for the great mother, my queen. If I kill you, I get rewarded with riches and gold," says Pilar.

He drops the sword and motions his fingers to come get it. She started to run with the dagger up on the side of her head screaming. When she got close to Benson, he reached for her arm and slammed her on the floor. He picked her up and the dagger and he put her on the chair and just tied her up. Once he did that, he ran up the stairs, but before he reached them, he tells her, "You're fired!" Then he started to run up the stairs. Once he reached the roof, Rebecca and Martha were knocked out.

"ALRIGHT BITCH! ENOUGH GAMES! LET'S END THIS ONCE AND FOR ALL!" yelled Benson. Daniel, who is still adjusting to his new powers, his eyes also have aura eyes so if she is invisible, he can see her. Then from out of nowhere Akasha came falling down missing Daniel.

Bricks broke and dust was all over the place. As she was standing up, she says to Daniel, "YOU STUPID LITTLE MAN! SINCE YOU HAVE GOT POWERS, LET'S SEE HOW YOU USE THEM. BECAUSE ONCE I KILL YOU, I'M GONNA KILL THAT CUNT WIFE OF YOURS AND THAT EVIL WITCH BITCH! YOU RUINED EVERYTHING!"

Akasha yelled at Daniel. As soon as she did that, Akasha began to change. She ripped off her clothes and her body began to deform into a creature like a pet then once she got done changing into a different form, she became a big black cat. She swiped her big paw and claws at Daniel but he ducked in time missing them "COME ON PUSSY!" he yelled at her Akasha turned again facing him this time Daniel was running towards her this time Akasha caught him with her claws and cut him right on in the front leaving big claw marks on his chest Daniel hissed at Akasha and she did the same to him they ran towards each other and they both jumped. They both caught each other so they was fighting up in the air Daniel punched her she swiped at his face he ducked but he was going To fall down so he grabbed her tail taking her down with him as they was going down at a fast pace Akasha form kicked Benson using her back paw as he was still holding on to her tail she tried to kick him off her tail as soon they hit the warehouse they made a big hole in the roof and then they went back inside the building. They both hit the floor hard. Benson was starting to get up feeling groggy from the fall he saw Akasha she went back to her normal form he walked straight up to her he went and took out the dagger out of his trench coat pocket he was about to stab her till she got up and grabbed him by the neck picking him off of the ground. Daniel tried to stab her but couldn't reach her cause her arms are so long as she was getting close to his face exposing her fangs, he still couldn't reach so he did the next best thing. He poked her eyes out and Akasha dropped Daniel. As she was trying to cover her eyes to adjust them as she was screaming.

"Thank you, three stooges." says Daniel as he was getting up. He started running towards her when she got her sight back. She went invisible just in time. "Okay Daniel, you got this. Just focus and readjust." he told himself. Once he got adjusted and his eyes settled, he tried to see her aura. Then from out of nowhere, she came up quick as she was in her black cat form again. She was hissing and growling at Daniel. He took one deep breath in and took a deep breath out. She was getting ready to pounce on Benson, but he moved. He grabbed her tail again and this time he swung Akasha over his head in circles. Then Benson slammed her on the brick wall, then she landed hard on the floor. With Daniel's powers he then ran fast toward her and got on top of her. He started choking her. Akasha's cat form did try to do one last attack; she swiped her claws at Daniel scratching his face. He got off her feeling his face. Benson turned around facing away from her, she got up on all fours. She pounced at Benson again with her claws out ready to end him. He managed to turn around and finally stab her before she could touch him. He used the dagger his dad gave to Quinn.

The cat hissed loudly as she fell to the ground. As she was slowly transforming back to her normal form, she screamed out to Benson. "YOU STUPID FOOL! HOW DARE YOU! ONCE A THOUSAND YEARS HITS, I SHALL RULE THE WORLD AGAIN! AAAAHHH!" Akasha then turned to stone.

Once Benson saw, he went for his shotgun. As he was about to shoot Akasha, a voice behind him made him stop.

"BROTHER STOP!"

Chapter Twenty

As Benson turned around it was his sister, Val, who was wearing a red robe covering her face and hands along with a few other people. All of them were wearing some gold medallion around their necks.

"Val? What the hell are you doing here? I thought I told you to leave town? How the hell did you find me?

"Your friend Martha, she called us and let us know the prophet one is here." says Val as she was uncovering her face. Just then Rebecca and Martha were coming down the stairs. Rebecca held Leah, who was still unconscious. Benson turned around and saw his wife and kid. He ran straight towards them.

"Is she still alive?" he asks Rebecca. She just nodded yes as she was crying. Just then Rebecca handed off Leah to Daniel.

"Baby, come on baby. It's me, daddy. wake up please, wake up" Daniel was telling Leah. "Val, what did this mega bitch do to her?" asks Benson.

Val and the rest of the red robe people were making their way to Daniel, and they were all speaking tongue. After they got done with what they were doing Val tells Daniel, "I'm sorry brother, but if she drank Akasha's blood, Akasha has her soul now. the only thing we can do is put her in our underground lab and just watch over her till Leah wakes up."

Benson, who wanted to cry, tells Val, "She was forced to drink the blood. So, she won't be my little girl anymore? She will be a monster now?"

Rebecca walked up next to Daniel and Leah. Rebecca started to rub Leah's hair and then started singing her favorite song, hoping she would wake up. It was no use. A few more red robe people started to make their way inside the warehouse just to take Akasha's body to be kept locked up and they took Pilar as well. She was just starting to come to from the hit Benson gave her.

"Brother, we have to take Leah. If we can cure her, she can be a normal little girl again. Just please let us take her and please help us fight these freak vampires.' says Val.

Daniel looked at Leah and then at Rebecca. From being married to a strong Irish woman you know what is right and wrong and she was right on this one. They both grinned and when Daniel turned his head back to his sister, he gave Leah to Val.

"Can I go with you?" Rebecca asks Val.

Val nodded yes and Val took Leah to some other red robe people and Rebecca went with them. Martha then came next to Daniel all messy and bloody.

"Are you okay?" she asked him. He just nodded yes. "Here, I found this on the father." she says, and it was the flask that Daniel gave O'Malley.

"Is it full?" he asks Martha.

"No." she says.

Benson just laughed and said, "That son of bitch. Hope he is burning in hell." he says.

"Are you ready to help us?" Val asks Daniel.

"First off, who are you for real? And second, what happened to your bar? And third, did dad know about this?" he asks her.

"First, we are called the 'Invictus society'. we are a group that hunts and kills vampires and werewolves and demons, second that guy that came in it was closing time I tell him we were closed and then he asks for my name and if you were my brother and all hell broke loose so I stabbed him in the heart and third dad knew. Dad always knew. He just kept it a secret from you, and he never knew you were or are a dhampir vampire." Val tells Daniel.

Benson, who was just sinking it all in, had to think it over for a minute. "Martha are these good people? can you trust them?" he asks her.

"Yes, because I'm a member, so don't worry. I'm a good witch and I can live forever too." says Martha.

After some thinking Daniel took the offer to be with the Invictus society.

"Good brother you can trust us and trust me I promise I'll watch over Leah" Val says to Daniel

"So, what is my first assessment with you guys?" he asks Val as Val was digging through her robe to give him an envelope to hand over to Daniel. Once Benson got the envelope, he opened it up and it was just a picture with two people in it.

Daniel, who had a shocked look on his face, tells Val, "I thought they were dead?" He says.

"No, people think they are dead, but they are not. They made a deal with the Six vampires. Come brother, your boat leaves in two hours for Paris, France." she tells Daniel and Benson nodded. He dropped down the picture on the floor and in that picture was none other than the gangster couple, Bonnie and Clyde.

95

EPILOGUE

Paris, France. The famous gangster couple Bonnie and Clyde chased after a poor defenseless woman.

After they catch up to her, Clyde tells Bonnie. "Go right ahead baby, ladies first. You know how I love to watch."

Just as Bonnie was about to bite into the woman's neck, they both heard a noise of a bottle being broken.

"Let the woman go!"

"Who's there? I'll bite you too!" says Clyde after Bonnie let the woman go, she was curious on who was with them.

"Who are you? Come on out, show yourself. We are hungry and we need to feast." Bonnie says.

Just then, a mysterious figure came from out of the darkness, it was Benson, with a new look. He leaned his body against the lamppost while smoking a cigar and wearing a new suit, sunglasses and still wearing his dad's lucky Fondra hat.

"Bonnie and Clyde, I have been looking for the two of you." he said as he was puffing on his cigar.

"Foolish human. You can't stop us! We made a deal with the Six Gods of vampires. We will live forever," says Clyde.

"Yeah, whatever my baby says, I agree with him now. Who are you? So, we can tell your family about how good you were." Bonnie says to Benson.

After Daniel got done smoking his cigar, he threw it on the ground. He lifted his body off of the light pole and he was hiding a weapon behind the shadows so Bonnie and Clyde wouldn't see. It's supposed to kill vampires.

He took off his sunglasses revealing his glowing red eyes and said, "The name is Benson, Daniel Benson, dhampir vampire hunter." He tells Bonnie and Clyde as he points his weapon at them. Bonnie and Clyde ran towards Benson while shrieking at him.

Catch Benson on his next adventure!

Acknowledgements

First, I would like to acknowledge the Lord Father God and Jesus Christ for blessing me to be on this earth every day.

Next, I would like to acknowledge all the college professors for giving me the experience and helping me with what I need to do with my book.

I would like to acknowledge my awesome editor, Felicia Witte, without her my book would not have been what it is today.

Next, I would like to thank my family. My dad Willie, my sister Valerie, and my brother Willie Ben, my brother in-law Joey and sister in-law Misty, my uncle Pete and aunt Sylvia. My numerous nephews and niece, great nephews, and great nieces. And my dog Harley.

Next I want to thank my awesome support system; Andrea L, Carla M, Robert H, Mariah E, Ally Y, Martha K, Rayne W, April T, Trina M, Terrianne P, and last but certainly not least Pilar S, and Deedra R. Thank you for kicking my butt and for making me keep going. Without you all I would not be here today. All your support and inspiration has gotten me this far and I hope I can only make you all proud.

Draft2Digital for making this a painless process.

If I forgot anyone, I do apologize.

Thank you to all the publishers for the offers.

Lastly, I want to thank all the formidable readers who have read my first book ever and I hope you have enjoyed it.

About the Author

Markus Danielson has found his true calling and passion. He enjoys writing short stories, movie scripts, or wrestling promos. He has finally found his true calling and passion. Markus Danielson is born and raised in Colorado. Whenever he is not writing, you can catch him playing video games, hanging out with his friends or family, or his fur daughter Harley. He has a winter home in Arizona and a summer home in Montana where he does most if his writing.